DALLAS AND THE COWBOY

LINDA GOODNIGHT

CHAPTER 1

*H*er day couldn't get any worse. In fact, her *life* couldn't get any worse.

Inside the manager's office of KVXN radio, Dallas Langley gripped the arms of the chair until her fingertips ached. For once, her perfectionist brain ignored the clutter and dirty coffee cups on her boss's desk.

A headache threatened at the back of her eyes.

She forcibly relaxed her death grip on the chair. *Calm down. Don't stress. You can't handle another migraine.* The third one since—

She slammed her eyes shut, and along with them, a mental door. No use thinking about that. She couldn't change it, no matter how many times she'd prayed to wake up from the horror.

And now this…

"You're firing me?" Amazing how sensible she sounded. Smooth voice, unruffled demeanor while she bled on the inside. That was Dallas Langley in a nutshell.

"Don't look at it that way." Jay Wallis's bushy gray eyebrows drew together in sympathetic consternation. He hated this. She knew he did. But he was doing it anyway.

"How else am I to look it, Jay? Fired is fired."

He lifted a hand, conciliatory. "Consider this an extended leave of absence. You've had a difficult month. You need more time. A week wasn't enough."

The week had turned her into a jumpy, irritable, OCD basket case. What she needed was work. What she needed was to be too busy to think about that awful night.

"I'm fine. Really."

Who was she kidding? She was a wreck. She hadn't had a full eight hours sleep in three weeks. The only thing that kept her sane was those hours behind the microphone focused on her listeners' problems instead of her own.

"*Dallas after Dark* is top-rated," she said. "Listeners love it. The warm, friendly talk, the gentle, common-sense advice, the tunes I spin just for them." She leaned in, earnest, persuasive. And ready to jump over the desk and throttle the man. "I need this job, and I'm the best you've got. You said yourself, syndication is in my future."

"Maybe when things die down..." He paused, winced.

Die down. Bad choice of words.

Dallas sat back in the chair, stomach churning, and wished for the millionth time she'd never taken that call. But Aaron had fooled her, and she'd answered. Now, every time she sat behind the mic staring at the blinking light on the call-in phone, her fingers trembled and her mouth went dry. Admittedly, her on-air conversation wasn't as breezy as before, but she'd get back to her old self. As long as she was working.

"You *were* the best. No denial from me," Jay said. "But the advertisers are spooked."

"Of my show? Or of me?" Her heart banged like a battering ram. Another few minutes and it would burst right out and bleed all over his desk. "None of this was my fault, Jay. I had no way of knowing Aaron would—"

"I know. I know." Jay said. "No one blames you."

Sure they did. Why else would a successful radio host suddenly become a pariah?

Hadn't the police questioned her for hours? Hadn't local news media run story after story about her and Aaron, carefully implying she must have done *something?*

And didn't she ask herself the same questions? Could she have done anything, said anything, to prevent the tragedy? Guilt was a funny emotion. It snuck up on her, pecked at her conscience like a drippy faucet and hinted that maybe, just maybe, she was to blame.

Jay, his fleshy face sad, handed an envelope across the desk. "Two weeks' severance and a little extra until you can find something else. I'm sorry, Dallas."

Her last, best hope crashed like waves in a hurricane. Severance. Not a leave of absence.

Jay was a good guy, a fair boss. He liked her, had let her have free rein with her show, her brainchild, her baby. And his radio station had flourished along with her popularity.

She wanted to say she understood, that she didn't blame him. After all, he was losing a lucrative show, a good host, a ton of advertising money. But right now, she was all out of sympathy. Between Station KVXN and the local police, she'd been let down about as much as she could stand.

Hot with humiliation and wounded to the core,

Dallas took the envelope and forced stiff legs to carry her out of his office and down the short hall, past the engineer, past the *On-Air* sign and the other offices, to the space she shared with the afternoon radio host.

The fact that Tessa Edwards was already in the office this early in the morning surprised Dallas. It shouldn't have. After the month she'd had, nothing should ever surprise her again.

Tessa spun the rolling chair away from her laptop to face Dallas. She didn't look her usual peppy self. "I'm sorry."

Dallas froze in the doorway and blinked, dumbfounded. "You knew?"

"He asked me to take your slot."

Already replaced? Seriously? Tessa was young and too pretty to be hidden behind a microphone, but underneath her long black weave was one smart chick with a lot of ambition. Yet, none of this was her fault.

Somehow Dallas managed a smile. It felt tiny and wimpy, but it was there. "You'll be awesome."

Tessa's shoulders relaxed. "I don't know how you do it. Grace under pressure. But thanks for understanding."

Grace under pressure? Not even close. Her heart

was bleeding all over the place. But she'd learned years ago about keeping the worst pain to herself. Once upon a time, she'd jump on horse, take a wild ride, and let the wind erase her tears. But she didn't have a horse anymore.

She didn't have a job either.

"I need to clear out my desk, then I'll be out of your way."

The thought was a hot spear through her chest… and through her dreams. This job had been the beginning. Syndication companies were already sniffing around. Or had been.

"You had a call while you were…in with Jay."

A call.

The awful dread hit the pit of her stomach. Acid boiled, threatening to eat her up. She took a deep breath, pressed a hand to her middle.

Stop. Just stop. Nothing's going to happen.

"Who was it?"

"Some guy named Wyatt something. Very serious. Deep, sexy voice. Sounded pretty hot. Is he your new man?"

Dallas never wanted another "new man." Ever. She stunk at choosing the right guy. Just like her mother had. Three stupid times.

"Never heard of him."

"He left a number, but said he'd call back in a while." Tessa ripped a sticky note from her desk and handed it over.

Dallas stared at the unfamiliar number. A reporter, maybe?

She folded the note and slid it into the pocket of her cardigan. No more reporters. They twisted everything she said, even when they were sympathetic.

After retrieving a cardboard box from storage, she sorted through the jetsam and flotsam in her desk. Three years was plenty of time to collect junk. All neatly organized, of course. She tossed most of it, keeping the personal items. When she came to the promo stuff, she balked. Pens, magnets, bumper stickers, all bearing the *Dallas after Dark* name next to the KVXN's red fox logo.

But *Dallas after Dark* was no more.

The lump in her chest rose to her throat and threatened to make her eyes water.

She left the promo items right where they were. They weren't hers. Not anymore.

The landline jingled. Dallas ignored it.

Tessa answered, then put her hand over the mouthpiece and whispered, "It's him."

Dallas frowned. "Him who?"

"Wyatt Caldwell, the guy who called before." She held out the receiver.

Dallas took the phone, prepared to hang up at the first indication she was being interviewed.

"This is Dallas."

"Dallas Langley? I'm Wyatt Caldwell."

A radio personality always noticed a voice. Tessa was right. This man had a voice to remember. Quiet, commanding, confident. Not that she'd be swayed by that.

Her jaw tightened. "Are you a reporter?"

A short pause. "No, ma'am."

She waited, not willing to give him anything. Reporters had lied to her before. But they hadn't called her ma'am.

"I'm—not sure how to say this, but"—she heard him suck air—"I think you're my sister."

SHERIFF LAWSON HAWK pulled the Ford Explorer to the speaker box of the Burger Barn drive-through. Calypso was quiet today, the way every small-town lawman preferred, a good thing after the Christmas fiasco with Marley Johnson. Lawson was a law-and-order man. Citizens paid him to keep the peace and protect them, even if one of their own was involved.

"The usual, Sheriff?" the disembodied voice asked.

Lawson couldn't help smiling. One of the blessings—and cursings—of a small town was that everyone knew him and his habits.

"Old fashioned," he said.

"Mustard and the works?"

"And fries, with a Coke."

"Cherry fried pie today, Sheriff? Aunt Mint made fresh ones about an hour ago."

"Sure. Toss one in." The voice he didn't recognize even knew his pie preference.

"You got it. I'll have your total at the window."

Lawson pulled the department Explorer to the next window as a small red SUV flashed past on the parallel street.

He glanced at his dashboard radar. Sixty. In a thirty-five. Somebody was in a hurry. His little town of Calypso, Texas, didn't need some speedster blasting through the streets, endangering motorists and pedestrians alike.

With no city police in sight, he hit the lights and siren and wheeled out of the Burger Barn drive-through, his juicy burger and crispy fries left behind. He'd settle up with Aunt Mint later. They'd played this scene before.

The snazzy red Chevy Equinox was escaping. From him.

It sailed through the green light, which turned yellow and then red before Lawson got there. He slammed on his brakes, skidded to a crawl.

Countess Belinda von Dunenburg exited the corner Hair Port Salon and gave him a questioning look.

Lawson checked left, then right, and stomped the accelerator. The big SUV bit pavement and left a trail of rubber.

Crazy fool driver was going to hurt someone. This was a small town, quiet and boring most of the time. Passers-through seemed to think they were under no obligation to obey school zone flashers or reduced speed limits.

Down the short main street and past the pastel colored businesses, locals pulled to the side of the street to let him pass. At the first convenience store, the little Chevy speedster skidded to a pause, whipped in, and stopped at the side of the building.

Vehicle still rocking, the driver's door slammed open.

A woman in a straight skirt with long, shapely legs Lawson tried to ignore jumped out and made a beeline for the door marked, *Women*. She got half way there, bent double, and lost her lunch.

Oh. She was sick. Not that being sick was an excuse for driving like a maniac, but still, he could be a little sympathetic. As long as she wasn't intoxicated. Lawson showed no mercy for anyone driving under the influence.

He pulled into the parking space next to the shiny red Equinox, put his vehicle in park, and considered. Should he offer assistance before or after he gave her a ticket?

She heaved again.

Definitely before.

Grabbing rubber gloves and wet wipes, he exited the vehicle and approached the woman. By now, she leaned against the gas station wall, holding her head. It was a pretty head. Sleek blonde hair to her shoulders with a classy cut and highlights that looked expensive. Except for the damp ends that could only mean one thing, given her recent bout of vomiting.

"Ma'am? Do you need assistance?" He stepped up on the walkway.

She swayed. Reached for the wall. Missed and started down. Lawson grabbed for her. The wet wipes thudded to the concrete.

She slumped, crumpling right into his arms.

Lawson took her weight, which wasn't much but enough to make him brace. His arms closed around her. She was soft and smelled...expensive, which was a relief, considering.

"Do you need an ambulance?" Though, in his current position with her taking up both arms, he couldn't reach his radio.

"I'm fine." The words were barely a whisper. Clearly, she was not fine...health-wise. The rest of her, however, was fine, indeed.

She tried to stand, moaned, reached for her head, and started down again.

Lawson did the only thing left to do. He gathered her up like a baby and carried her to her car. In her rush, she'd left the door open. It was cold today, stinking cold, but the car's interior still felt warm.

Once she was settled in the seat, she slumped forward, head against the steering wheel, and moaned again. She was in no position to drive, so he considered the options. Take her to emergency care himself or call an ambulance.

Removing the radio from his belt, he pushed for dispatch and asked for an ambulance.

"Sorry, Sheriff," Sandra said. "The ambulance is on a run. Heart attack out in the canyons. It might be a while."

Lawson signed off, scooped the sick woman up again, and carried her to his vehicle. After depositing her in the backseat, he grabbed her purse and keys, locked her car, and headed toward the Calypso Medical Center.

DALLAS WAS AWARE OF VOICES, movement. And movement made her nauseous. She moaned or thought she did. Where was she?

Someone forced an eyelid up. Shined a light into her pupils. She jerked her face to one side and squeezed her eyes shut. The motion shot excruciating pain through the back of her head.

Something tight pinched at her index fingertip. Someone lifted her arm, applied a cuff. She heard a hissing noise.

Was she in a hospital?

Conversation around her continued, but she couldn't make out the words. Her head hurt too much. Welcoming the darkness, she let the thoughts fade.

"Miss Langley? Dallas?" A man's voice poked at her peace. Hands patted her arm. She felt a stick, jerked. "Dallas, try to hold still. We're starting an IV." Definitely a hospital. "Can you tell us what happened?"

Must be a doctor.

Though her mouth tasted like sticky sewer, she managed to part her lips and murmur, "Migraine. Basilar."

Several voices reacted at once, and she could feel activity all around the hard bed.

"We'll give you something for that. What meds do you usually take?"

She struggled past the dizziness and nausea but was saved from speaking when a man's familiar voice answered for her. "I brought her handbag. She has a prescription bottle in there along with ID."

She thought about protesting this clear invasion of her person but didn't have the energy.

"The bottle is empty," the same man said.

Dallas frowned, or thought she did. Where had she heard that voice before?

"When did you last take your medication?" The doctor again. Or maybe a nurse.

She managed a whisper. "Yesterday." At least, she thought it had been yesterday. Everything was fuzzy and painful right now.

A hand patted her. The doctor person, a comforter with soft, warm hands. The other man's hands had been warm, too, but strong and tough.

"Just relax, Dallas. The nurse will put some medication through your IV and have you feeling better soon."

The nurse must have been quick, because that was the last thing Dallas remembered.

SHE AWOKE in a thankfully dark room, window drapes closed. Only a faint crack between the curtains that were parallel to her bed allowed in light. Her head still hurt but not as badly. She'd regained her eyesight, and the nausea had lessened.

What time was it?

Lifting a hand, she saw the IV. Her arm seemed to weigh a thousand pounds. She'd been this route before. ER, an exam room to sleep off the pain, and sometimes a hospital bed. Apparently, she was still in an exam room.

The curtain parted, and a male nurse in dark blue scrubs entered. Dallas closed her eyes against the inevitable light but shifted slightly to let the nurse know she was awake.

"Miss Langley." The man spoke quietly. "I need to take your vitals."

Dallas managed to move her lips. "Okay."

He applied a blood pressure cuff. "Is the pain any better?"

"Yes."

"On a scale of one to ten, with ten being the worst, can you rate your current pain?"

"Six." If she didn't move too much.

The man completed his check and started out of the cubicle. "I'll let Doctor Marsh know. Sheriff Lawson, too. He asked to be kept apprised."

"Sheriff?" Was she in trouble?

But the nurse was already gone.

INSIDE THE DELICIOUSLY-SCENTED confines of the Burger Barn, Lawson took a huge bite of his old-fashioned burger, attempting once again to have his lunch. Which was now long past, so the homemade burger was probably dinner.

Double meat on a well-grilled bun and loaded with veggies set his taste buds dancing. He took another bite and then another, suddenly aware of how hungry he was. Had he skipped breakfast again? Probably. That was about the time the call came in about the rabid skunk in Hannah Richards's barn.

Aunt Mint, an Amazonian-sized woman who owned the popular Burger Barn hang-out, stopped by his table. "Marley and Wyatt were in earlier. Glad things worked out with them."

"Me, too." Wyatt, like all the Caldwells, was a close friend. Arresting his fiancé had been among the harder things Lawson had ever had to do. "Relieved she was innocent."

He looked fondly at this burger. Aunt Mint, who wasn't anyone's aunt that he knew of, patted his back and chuckled. "I'll leave you to your food. You look hungry."

"Could use that cherry pie I missed out on earlier." A Burger Barn specialty, fried pies, made fresh every day. Reminded him of Pie Town over in Refuge, also in his jurisdiction. He stopped in when he could but lately he was so busy patrolling the whole county, he had little time to spare. He needed an undersheriff to take some of the load off.

"You got it."

As she walked away, his cell phone vibrated against his hip. He answered. "Sheriff Hawk."

"Hey, big brother, how's it going?" The voice on the other end was exceptionally cheerful.

Lawson's burger lost its taste. He barely knew his half brother, but one thing he did know. Bryce Addington never called unless he wanted something. The last time had cost Lawson several thousand dollars. Yeah, he was stupid like that sometimes. But not this time.

"What's up, Bryce?" He tried to keep his tone civil. After all, Bryce was his mother's son, even if they'd been raised in different states by different dads.

"Couldn't be better. I got this deal going in Nashville, and it sounds like the big boys are ready to listen."

"Glad to hear it. Good luck." Bryce had dreams of fame and fortune. Sure, he was a halfway decent guitar picker and could carry a tune, but so were thousands of other hopefuls with a better work ethic. "Are you in Nashville now?"

"Well, see that's the problem…"

Lawson raised his eyes to the ceiling. *Here it comes.*

"I can't take Madison with me, so I thought, hey, I got a brother. He barely knows his only flesh-and-blood niece, so I was wondering if she could stay with you."

"With me? You can't be serious."

"As brain surgery. Come on, bro, she won't be any trouble. Great kid. A real sweetheart. Old enough to be a help around your place. If I don't go now I'll miss my shot."

"What about her mother?"

"Sherry's long gone. Don't know where she is. Abandoned us." He tried to sound pitiful. "It's just me and my sweet baby girl doing our best to make ends meet."

Lawson wasn't buying this latest con job. "Can't. Sorry."

"Hey! At least hear me out." Bryce's tone changed to anger. "What kind of man are you if you don't help your only brother?"

Hackles rose on the back of Lawson's neck. "The kind who thinks you need to get your act together, and I don't mean your singing act. Grow up, take responsibility for your life—and for your daughter."

"You're a real jerk, you know that?" Bryce's tone changed to a sneer. "And you call yourself a Christian."

Lawson hung up on him and sat there staring at the cell phone, fuming. Mad because Bryce never failed to put him in a spot. Furious because he felt guilty for saying no.

The cell phone buzzed. He jumped and squinted at the number. Not Bryce. With a longing look at his burger, he let out a frustrated hiss, and answered.

"Sheriff Hawk."

"Nurse Brent Fielding here, Sheriff. The woman you brought to the ER is awake."

Lawson made the inner switch from aggravated brother to concerned lawman. "She better?"

"Some. Doc wants to keep her overnight and make sure her meds are working."

"Good. What room?"

"Don't know yet. Check at the front desk."

"Will do." He hung up, finished his burger, took his pie with him, and headed toward the hospital.

Dallas Langley still had a ticket coming.

CHAPTER 2

*S*he was asleep.

Lawson stood at the foot of the woman's bed and fought a most unprofessional urge to smooth the tangled blond hair away from her cheek. She looked small and vulnerable. Pale, too.

She moaned, a frown pinching her features. He stepped forward to... He didn't know what he'd planned to do. Be there. Reassure her.

He dragged a hand over his face. *Man.* If just watching a pretty woman sleep sent him down romantic rabbit trails, he needed to date more. He'd never experienced such an undeniable jolt of emotion toward anyone.

Sleeping Beauty didn't have nothing on this lady.

He watched the rise and fall of her chest beneath

the white sheet as she settled once more, her face smoothing into relaxation. Doc was keeping her overnight. Good. Lawson didn't want her on the road.

He wondered where she was headed and had the odd thought that he hoped it was somewhere close to Calypso.

When she didn't awake, he eased out. The ticket could wait.

THE REST of the day kept Lawson busy, but thoughts of a pale face and blond hair were never far away.

He transported a prisoner for the town police, made a run out to the county line where someone had shot a rancher's cow, and then rounded up a herd of horses that had gotten loose. By the time he found the owners, the sky was dark and he was worn slick.

With the horse owner's thanks ringing in his head, he called it a day and aimed the Explorer home. All he wanted to do was head to his peaceful little ranch on the edge of town, feed his horses, watch a little basketball on TV, and tumble into bed. The deputies would handle the night shift.

The law dog in him kept an eye on things as he

passed his neighbors. When his headlights illumi-
nated his mailbox, he stopped for his mail, tossed it
on the seat, and pulled down the short drive. The
ranch-style house wasn't big, but a confirmed bachelor didn't need much. A nice-sized living and
kitchen combo for entertaining friends. Three
bedrooms in case he had guests, which he never did,
but who bought a one-bedroom ranch? The thirty
acres were what he loved. A place for his horses, a
big barn and corrals, a storage building.

His headlights washed across the front porch. He
blinked, slowed the car, leaned forward, and
squinted. Somebody sat on the steps.

Lawson touched the weapon at his hip. He was
well liked in the county, but every officer of the law
made enemies.

As he drove closer, the figure rose. A kid. His
belly dropped as suspicion grew. He'd only seen her
a couple of times, and she'd been a lot smaller, but it
had to be her. Madison. His niece. Bryce's daughter.

If he wasn't a law-and-order guy, he'd be tempted
to murder his half-brother—who was nowhere in
sight.

He parked the vehicle beside the porch and got
out. The girl stood. A backpack lay on the step.

"Madison?"

"Yeah. Your favorite niece. Aren't you thrilled to see me?" Her tone was resentful, as if her sudden, unexpected appearance was his fault.

"What's going on? I thought you were headed to Nashville with your dad." What else was he to think after he'd flat out refused to babysit?

"Not too smart on your part if you believed that." She hitched up the backpack. "Can we go in? I'm cold."

Of course, she was. Temp had dropped at least ten degrees since sundown.

He unlocked the door, clicked on the lights. "Where's your dad?"

"Halfway to the promised land, I guess." She dropped the backpack and shrugged out of a dirty pink puffer jacket.

The kid would have been pretty without the belligerent expression. Big gray eyes, tilted nose, and smooth skin not yet tormented with acne. Pale blonde hair that reminded him of Dallas Langley, only Madison's looked none too clean and was yanked back in a messy tail with multiple strands stringing around her face. She wore the typical middle-school gear. Tennis shoes, jeans, and a hoodie emblazoned with the slogan, *#Idon'tcare*.

The attitude did not encourage him.

"The promise land being Music City?" he asked.

"Oh, yeah." She moved around his living room, taking in the sights, her voice a mixture of disinterest and sarcasm. "He's gonna make it big this time. Buy a house. Get me a car. Whoopee."

"You're too young to drive."

She looked at him over one shoulder. "Tell that to him. I've been driving since I was ten."

Lawson cringed. "What are you now?"

"Thirteen."

Thirteen and full of insolence. Where was the sweet, obedient child his brother had described? Probably the same place as the money his dear brother owed him. "How did you get here?"

She hiked a shoulder. "Hitched."

"You *what*?" Lawson thought his heart would stop. "Don't you know how dangerous that is? You should have called me."

She lifted a dubious eyebrow. "With what? The cell phone I don't have? And even if I'd borrowed one, would you have come? I have ears. I heard him talking to you."

She had him there. "Your dad just dumped you out and left you to catch a ride?"

"I've done it before. No big deal. Truckers are usually nice."

Lawson thought he'd swallow his tonsils. Hitchhiking. A thirteen-year-old girl. Was she nuts? And what was he supposed to do with her? He knew about as much about belligerent teenage girls as he knew about ballet dancing. Nothing.

"You hungry?"

Again, the nonchalant shrug. "I could eat. You cooking?"

"Looks that way."

With a longing glance toward his recliner, Lawson headed to the kitchen and the refrigerator. While taking out bacon and eggs, he motioned toward the hallway.

"Put your backpack in the extra bedroom while I rustle up some food. Down the hall, at the end. Bathroom's across from it."

"So I'm staying?"

"For tonight." Until he could figure out what to do. His irresponsible brother better get his head together quick.

"He won't answer if you call. And I'm not going to foster care."

Lawson slapped a skillet on the stove and turned to face her. "He's done this before?"

"What do you think? He's not exactly father of the year."

So cynical for such a young kid. Lawson found that his compassion gene, which was considerable, had started to ache. Madison slouched in the kitchen doorway, pretending to be tough when she had to be crying inside. Rejection stunk, and apparently, she'd been hurt too many times.

"Tough day?" he asked softly.

She bristled. "I didn't ask you to feel sorry for me. I just wanted to be clear. I'm not going to foster care. So if you've got any funny ideas about dumping me—"

Lawson lifted a hand, cut her off. "Got it."

She whipped around and tromped down the hall, dragging the backpack and mad at the world. Lawson got busy frying bacon and eggs, pondering this unexpected turn of events.

By the time the food was ready, Madison still hadn't returned. Lawson stuck his head in the hallway and yelled, "Supper's on."

He plopped plates on the small square table for two, added a few condiments and the food along with glasses of milk.

Madison reappeared in the kitchen doorway. Her hair dripped water onto a blue sweater, her face shiny and pink. "I took a shower. You're out of shampoo."

She glared at Lawson as though he'd complain. He motioned toward a chair. "Sit. Supper's on."

She sat and reached for the food platter, scraping half the six eggs and half the bacon onto her plate. She didn't bother with salt or pepper or ketchup or hot sauce the way he would. She dug in, shoveling food like a teenage backhoe.

Lawson filled his plate, bowed his head, and said a quiet prayer of thanks, though inside he was praying for guidance. And patience. When he lifted his head, Madison was staring at him, chewing away. Two of the eggs were already gone. She gulped a long swallow of milk.

"Been a while since breakfast?" he asked casually.

"Yeah. Like in yesterday. I figured I'd better save my money in case…"

Lawson didn't even want to know the rest. "Eat all you want. There's plenty."

"This is enough."

He scraped another egg onto her plate anyway. She ate it.

When she finally slowed down, she fiddled with a piece of toast and said, "Are you an Indian?"

Lawson blinked. This kid was full of surprises. "Why do you ask?"

"You don't look like one."

"What do you think an Indian looks like?"

"I don't know. Like on TV, I guess. Dad said you were. Said you'd scalp me if I didn't behave." She studied him like a specimen. "But I don't see it."

The law be hanged. He really *was* going to throttle his brother. "Why not?"

"Your eyes are blue."

He snorted. "You ever heard of rude stereotypes?"

"People are what they are. Why would I care?" She nailed him with those gray eyes. "So. Are you?"

"Native American? Which, by the way, is the preferred term. Yes, I am. Partly. Along with a strong dose of your grandmother's Scots-Irish. My father was half Chickasaw." And Lawson was proud of that heritage.

"So you're what? Like, a quarter or something?"

He nodded. The quarter was enough to give him a good tan and dark hair, and that was about it. "Yes, and you're quick with the math."

"Not rocket science." She shoved a chunk of toast in her mouth.

"Word to the wise. Don't go around boldly asking questions about someone's ethnicity. People are sensitive about that stuff."

"Why? If you're proud of it. I wish I knew what I was."

Lawson lifted his milk glass. "Space alien, maybe?"

The kid almost laughed, but she managed to hold it in.

They ate the rest of the meal in relative silence, which suited Lawson. He was too tired and disgruntled to carry on a decent conversation.

He finished one egg and a couple slices of bacon while she devoured every crumb on her plate and gulped down two glasses of milk. She wasn't big. Maybe five feet and a hundred pounds. Where she put the food was anyone's guess.

When Madison pushed her plate away and let out a long sigh, Lawson began clearing the table. He wasn't a man to leave his dishes undone. After all, no one else was around to do them. So, he ran the dish water and got busy. Behind him, he heard the fridge door open and glanced over his shoulder. Madison was putting away the butter and jelly and his beloved ketchup. She caught him looking, slammed the door, and stalked out of the room. The bottles inside the refrigerator rattled.

Lawson growled and scrubbed harder on the frying pan.

He wasn't cut out to babysit a teenager.

What was he going to do with her if Bryce refused to return? Even though Calypso County's very own foster and adoption specialist, Emily Caldwell Donley, would see to it she had a good placement, Lawson wouldn't send his niece to foster care, not when she was so opposed. But he was a busy man and a bachelor. No women to advise him. What was he supposed to do with a snarky teenage girl?

Pulling the drain plug, he washed down the sink, dried his hands, and headed down the hall to the guest room, where he pecked lightly at the door.

"What?" came the sharp reply.

"May I come in?"

"It's your house."

He sighed and eased the door open. "A polite, 'come in' would be better."

She'd kicked off her shoes and lay on her side at the end of the full bed scribbling in a spiral notebook. She blinked up at him, expression annoyed. "What?"

So much for the manners lesson.

"I'm calling it a night. Is the room okay? Do you have everything you need? The chest and closet are empty if you want to use those."

She sat up, her face bewildered but edged with

hope. The kind of hope that stabbed Lawson in the heart. "Are you letting me stick around? Just till the old man comes for me, I mean. Probably won't be too long."

He hadn't decided yet. First, he and Bryce had to have a long talk. "Aren't you afraid I'll scalp you?"

Gray eyes widened. "Would you?"

He laughed, shaking his head. "No, Madison. I wouldn't. And that's an ugly stereotype we don't appreciate."

She offered the universal head roll that infuriated adults. "Gee, I'm sorry," she said in the most insincere apology ever. "You don't have to cry about it."

"Goodnight, Madison." He shut the bedroom door and started down the hall. Behind him, he heard the lock click. Probably afraid he'd scalp her. He shook his head and found his way to the bedroom that had been calling his name for hours.

Tomorrow, he had a lot on his agenda. Right now, he didn't want to think about work or angry teenagers or his irresponsible brother. He wanted to think of something or someone pleasant. A vision of blonde hair and a pretty face appeared behind his eyelids.

Dallas Langley.

Where was she from? Why she had she been flying through Calypso?

And why did she linger so strongly in his mind?

THE NEXT MORNING, Dallas wobbled to the bathroom to wash up and get dressed, grateful that someone had brought her overnight bag to the hospital. The headaches always interfered with her mental acuity and left her as washed out as a bleached red sock. She was in no shape to meet these Caldwell people who claimed to know her father. She wanted to be at her best, sharp, in case they wanted something from her that she wasn't willing to give. A person couldn't be too careful these days.

Wobbling back to the stiff, miserable hospital bed, she sat on the edge and tried to remember the course of events that had brought her to the ER. The phone call from Wyatt Caldwell, of course, which was one more shock in a long month of mental stresses. Then the decision to drive to this tiny town several hundred miles from Bayville, the growing headache, and the awareness of being so very, very sick, followed by a man with strong arms. She'd have to find him, thank him. Someone at the hospital would know who brought her in.

Dallas took her handbag from the nightstand and fished for her car keys. Not there. She reached for the nurse's call button to ask.

"I'm not sure, miss," came the reply. "But the sheriff is headed your way. Maybe he'll know."

The sheriff? Again? Had she wrecked the car? No. She was confident she hadn't. Had he, a *cop* no less, been her rescuer?

A knock sounded and after her weak, "Come in," a figure appeared in the doorway. A dark-haired, good-looking male figure. In a uniform. With a cowboy hat. Every female cell in her weak body went on red alert.

Even though he was a cop, Dallas was thrilled to have put on her makeup. Not that she looked her best, but she had to look better than she had yesterday.

Gear rattled as the cop approached. Muscles she didn't want to notice rippled when he removed his hat. He brought with him the smell of crisp cold air and a fresh shave. "How you feeling?"

"Alive." She managed a wan smile. "Are you the one who drove me to the ER?"

"Yes, ma'am."

"Thank you. And it's Dallas. Dallas Langley."

"Yes, ma'am. I'm Sheriff Lawson Hawk."

He just *had* to add the sheriff part. Show off his authority. Typical cop.

But the memory of strong arms and a warm chest came back to her. Comforting, secure. He'd taken care of her.

"You were in a bad spot yesterday," he said. "Is that a frequent occurrence?"

"'Bad spot' is a nice way of putting it." The man had seen her vomit, for crying out loud! "And to answer your question, the headaches have been especially bad lately."

She stopped short of saying more. No one, not one single person in this town, needed to know about Aaron. She didn't want the gossip and whispers to start again. Not that she planned to stick around long, but maybe she would. Anywhere except Bayville sounded perfect right now. People here had already proved to be kind and helpful, and she might actually have family here.

The sheriff helped himself to a chair and pulled it close to where she sat on the bed. The man was real eye candy, all black eyelashes and brilliant blue eyes with the right amount of masculine bone structure to keep him from looking feminine. That, and the fact that his body was honed and fit and about as masculine as any she'd ever admired.

And admire she did. Along with a completely unwanted but powerful jolt of attraction. Cops, even helpful, good-looking local sheriffs, were not on her happy list.

"I noticed your Texas tag. What part of Texas are you from?"

None of his pretty business. "Do you have my car keys?"

"I do." He dug the keys from his jacket and dangled them toward her. "You were in no condition to drive."

Her temper flared. "What was I going to do? Stop in the middle of the highway and just sit there until the headache passed?"

He gave her a mild look. "That's why I took the keys. You were too sick to drive yourself to the hospital. So I secured your car and drove you here."

"Oh." She snatched the outstretched fob. "Where's my car?"

"Pete's Quick Stop on the edge of town. Pete said he'd keep an eye on it until you're ready."

"I'm ready now."

The man didn't take the hint and move. And she was trapped between him and the hospital bed.

"You have folks in Calypso, or are you passing through?"

Was this an interrogation? "I'm in town to see someone."

His sapphire eyes studied her. He wanted to pry. She knew he did. But she wasn't telling him another thing. She didn't know the Caldwells, and even if they were kin, she wouldn't share such personal information with a stranger. Even a cop.

"Doc released you yet?"

"I'm waiting on a prescription. Then, I'll schedule an Uber."

"Not in Calypso you won't," he said.

"There are no Uber drivers in this town?" Really? She'd thought they were everywhere.

"Not a one. We have a single taxi, but you don't need to worry about that. I brought you here. I'll take you back to your car."

"Oh. Well. Thanks." A cop was going out of his way to be nice. Might as well take advantage of such a rare event.

Something banged against the door, and a nurse rolled a wheelchair inside. "Ready to get out of here?"

"More than ready." She pushed to her feet. Her ears began to buzz. Her knees wobbled. The incessant head throb started up again. "Oh."

Grappling for the bed behind her with one hand,

she tried to sit but missed her mark and grazed the mattress edge.

"Whoa, there." Strong hands caught her under the arms and brought her upright. "You sure you're ready for this?"

Dallas gave her head a slow shake. It thrummed, but not like yesterday. "Absolutely."

The sheriff, strong hands and flexed muscles, turned her toward the wheelchair and guided her down. The nurse put her handbag in her lap, and the lawman grabbed her overnight bag. "This everything?"

"Yes."

They rolled her out to the waiting police vehicle. The cop's gear bumped the edge of the wheelchair, his lean, uniformed legs in her peripheral vision. She'd never been more aware of the way a man walked, loose limbed and confident.

After he eased her onto the passenger seat, he pulled the seat belt toward her and smiled. "Buckle up."

The smile was deadly. White teeth, dark skin, sparkly blue eyes. Maybe the buzzing in her head wasn't from the headache after all.

He got in the driver's seat, and they started out of the hospital loading zone. "Where to?"

"My car?"

"I'm not sure you're ready to get behind the wheel."

"I'm perfectly capable—"

"Of passing out in the hospital room."

"I'm fine now."

"You said you were in town to see someone. I could drop you there." He raised both eyebrows, clearly curious.

"Just take me to my car and then direct me to a hotel. I can drive myself." The hotel was a great idea. Another day's rest would gear her up to phone Wyatt Caldwell.

Lawson Hawk made a completely male noise of disagreement but said no more. The man had no idea that she'd dealt with migraines most of her life. She knew the drill. She'd be weak and pathetic for a couple of days, maybe more, and then she'd bounce right back.

"Royal B & B in town is very nice, and we have a fairly new Best Western right off Main. I'm told it's clean and the rates are reasonable."

"The hotel works." Chatty bed-and-breakfast proprietors were not her thing, especially when she was battling a migraine.

In short order, they pulled into the convenience

store parking area. The sheriff killed the engine and turned toward her, one arm slung over the steering wheel. "Remember this?"

"Vaguely." Mostly she remembered him, his solid strength and kindness, and the awful pain. She reached for the door handle. "I don't know how to thank you enough—"

He lifted a hand. "No need. Part of the job."

Right. He hadn't rescued her out of the goodness of his heart. He was a cop, duty bound.

He came around and opened her door. Dallas stepped out. The embarrassing whirlwind started inside her head again. She wobbled, tried to gain her balance, but plopped back onto the seat. Her heart rattled and her breath came short.

"Maybe I should get that hotel room first."

CHAPTER 3

*L*awson was glad Dallas had finally caved about driving. He still owed her a ticket, which he hadn't quite been able to write out yet, but there was no way he wanted her behind the wheel of a car until she had her legs back under her. And okay, he'd admit it. He liked the idea of her sticking around town a few days.

He made small talk during the short drive, pointing out Main Street amenities, the doughnut shop, a diner, and a couple fast food places in case she got hungry.

"They're within walking distance of the hotel, but you can order in, too. Which I recommend."

"Why?" She turned, smiling.

She had a gorgeous smile. Fact of the matter, she

was more gorgeous today than she'd been yesterday. Which, he supposed, wasn't exactly a compliment.

"Think I'm too wimpy to walk a couple of blocks?"

He smiled back. "Really want me to answer that?"

A chuckle bubbled up. "No. But I do want you to know I'm normally a very strong, independent person."

"Duly noted. We all need a little help now and then."

She turned back toward the road, suddenly serious, and murmured, "Isn't that the truth?"

He'd been curious about her before. Now he wanted to know her. She intrigued him. Stirred him up a little too, and he hadn't let anyone stir him in a long time.

At the hotel, he nodded to Rod Brinks, the desk clerk, and stood close while Dallas, pale and shaky, checked in. She'd walked the few feet from the entrance where he'd parked, but he could see the effort had taken most of her strength. The meds the hospital had administered must have been powerful.

"Give her a first-floor room, Rod," Lawson said. "Miss Langley's been in the hospital."

Rod's bespeckled face wreathed in appropriate

DALLAS AND THE COWBOY

sympathy. "I'm sorry to hear that, ma'am. Is there anything special you'd like brought to your room?"

"Maybe some bottled water?"

With a smile, the clerk reached behind him into a small cooler and took out two bottles. "Here you go. Welcome to Best Western, Calypso."

Lawson reached in and took the water, hefted her bag, and followed her down the hall like a bell-man. A very watchful bellman. She's was doing pretty well, but he didn't want her fainting on him again.

At Room 5, Dallas paused to swipe the key. "Is this part of the job too, Sheriff? Delivering pathetic women to their hotel rooms?"

"Better than having them on my roads." He winked to let her know he kidded. Sort of.

The lock clicked, and she leaned her weight against the door. It didn't budge. Lawson reached around her and pushed.

She groaned. "Wimpy."

He grinned at her back and followed her in, sweeping the room with his eyes as he set the bag and water on the end of the bed. She sat next to them, clearly relieved to be off her feet.

"Anything I can do for you before I leave?"

"No." She offered a hand. Long slim fingers

clasped his. Soft fingers. "Thank you for everything, Sheriff. I'm sorry to be such a bother."

A rush of heat shot through Lawson's body as he gazed down into her face. He had the oddest desire to sit down beside her and learn everything there was to know about Dallas Langley. He wanted to listen to her voice, watch her talk, make her laugh.

Reluctantly, he withdrew his hand. Enough of this nonsense. Didn't he have enough female trouble at the moment?

"I'll stop by in the morning to take you to your car." He reached inside his jacket for the business cards he kept handy. "Call if I can be of further assistance."

Sounding and feeling stiff and a tad bit awkward, he exited the room.

DALLAS KICKED off her shoes and crawled onto the bed, propping two pillows at her back. She took a long drink from the water bottle and relaxed, the handsome sheriff in the front of her thoughts.

The hospital meds must have affected her thinking. Either that, or she was seriously crushing on a cop she'd barely met.

"Probably both," she muttered and tilted her head

back. A vague pulse tapped at the base of her skull, and she realized she hadn't had the prescription filled.

"Should be okay. I probably have enough meds in me to last a week." She hoped.

The last thing she wanted to do was leave this room. Just getting here had wiped her out. The ride had been pleasant, though, listening to the sheriff rumble about his town and the good people.

She'd almost asked him about Wyatt Caldwell. Almost. Maybe tomorrow, she would. He would know if the Caldwells were worth knowing. She still didn't know what she'd do if they were, indeed, kin. What did they want? Why would they be interested, at this point, in making contact with a half sister they'd never met? A half sister who probably meant their father had cheated on their mother. Not a pleasant thought.

"Half sister." She rolled the words through her mind. Yesterday, she'd been too shocked to thoroughly consider what this meant.

She probably should have called Mom, but she'd been afraid of hurting her. Stephanie Langley wasn't sensitive about much, but she'd always gotten upset anytime Dallas asked about her birth father.

The left side of Dallas's head started to thud

again. Stress was a trigger. And her stress wasn't going away any time soon.

LAWSON LEFT the hotel with Dallas's classy fragrance in his nostrils and an odd feeling in his chest. He'd also left the clerk with instructions--and a twenty-dollar gratuity—to check on Miss Langley's well-being in a few hours.

The rest of his morning was spent in paperwork and meetings, though two blond females weren't far from his thoughts.

He'd been uncertain about leaving Madison alone at the ranch, but when he'd said so, she'd scoffed. Bryce left her alone all the time, let her drive a car at his convenience and then hitchhike on the interstate. What harm could come to her at a ranch?

Now at his desk inside the courthouse, Lawson found a free minute to make contact with his half brother. No answer. He left a message. Thirty minutes later, he left another. When that didn't produce a response, he texted.

"Respond, or I'm filing child abandonment charges."

The reply was instantaneous. "I didn't abandon her. She's with her beloved uncle."

"She doesn't even know me."

"Time to get acquainted."

Lawson ground his back teeth. "She belongs with her father."

"She's better off with you."

He had a point. Bryce's half-homeless, totally irresponsible, vagabond lifestyle wasn't good for anyone.

"If she stays here, she needs to be in school."

"So enroll her."

In other words, Bryce had no intention of returning any time soon. Maybe never.

"Get back here ASAP!"

"Sure thing. Gotta run now."

Lawson texted a few more, terse commands but received no more answers. He shouldn't be surprised. Still, this was epic idiocy on Bryce's part. Maybe on his part too. After all, he'd just inherited someone else's problem.

His conscience twanged like a tuning fork. Madison wasn't a problem. She was a human being with thoughts and feelings, a confused, angry, wounded kid.

"Could use a little direction, Lord," he murmured. And then he shoved the cell phone into his pocket with enough force to rip the pocket.

At noon, he radioed his intention to dispatch, picked up a pizza, and cruised out to the ranch. He found Madison sprawled on his comfy old couch watching, surprisingly, a cooking show. When he came in, she didn't bother to get up. Just eyed him with enough suspicion and uncertainty to give his heart a pinch.

"Pizza," he said, holding up the brown-and-red cardboard box.

"Not pepperoni, I hope."

Struck out again. "You can take the pepperoni off, Madison. It's still a cheese pizza."

"I guess."

She followed him into the kitchen for a slice. And, he noticed with some glee, she did not toss the pepperoni.

"I talked to your dad today."

Gray eyes flashed at him. "No way."

"I'm an officer of the law. There's always a way to get people to talk."

"Oh." She shoved a bite in her mouth, letting the mozzarella string down her chin. "He's not coming, is he?"

Her resigned tone let him know exactly how little she expected from her father.

"You're staying with me for a while."

She reeled in the mozzarella. "And you are just thrilled out of your gourd."

He wasn't touching that remark with the famous ten-foot pole.

"Tomorrow, we'll get you enrolled in school." And begin laying some ground rules for life with the local sheriff.

Madison rolled her eyes and groaned but didn't argue.

His cell buzzed. He answered without looking. "Hawk here."

"Sheriff, this is Rob at Best Western. You said to call if the lady in room five, Miss Langley, needed anything."

"What's going on? Is she sick again?"

"Headache, I think. She asked me about getting a prescription filled but no one in town delivers. I'd go after it myself, but I can't leave the desk. She's going to walk to the pharmacy, but she looks kind of weak and sickly to me."

"Be there in a few. Thanks, Rob." He hung up, replaced the phone, and started for the door. If he left now, he could fill the script before his lunch hour ended. "Gotta get going."

As he started to exit the house, Madison called, "Hey!"

He pivoted. She came from the kitchen holding out a paper towel with two pizza slices. "You didn't eat."

The simple kindness felt like a giant step in the right direction.

IF SHE WASN'T CAREFUL, Dallas was going to change her mind about cops. At least about small-town, sheriff-type cops in cowboy hats.

He'd not only taken her to fill the prescription, he'd stopped at a local diner for a bowl of chicken soup with plenty of crackers. At her request, of course, but he could have said no. That he hadn't said a lot about him.

This was after he'd pulled alongside her and threatened to arrest her if she didn't get in the car and stop fainting on his sidewalks. She'd laughed and gratefully gotten in. Even though the pharmacy was only two blocks from the hotel, the ride was a big relief. She was the weakest she'd ever been after one of these episodes.

Currently, Lawson Hawk stood inside her hotel room door, hat in hand, looking too good to be a cop. He'd refused to sit, though there were two chairs. Professional distance, she supposed. And rightly so. What would his constituents think about him visiting a stranger in her hotel room? Gossip was the avocation of small towns and, often, larger ones. She was living proof.

"Do you always chauffer visitors?" she asked.

"Only those I find throwing up on my town's sidewalks."

She grimaced. "You didn't have to remind of me of that little indelicacy."

His eyes twinkled. "If the town makes you sick, we're obligated to look after you. City ordinance." But he smiled to let her know he joked.

Imagine that, a cop with a sense of humor.

"Give my thanks to the city. Not that Calypso is responsible for my migraines, but the hospitality is exceptional."

"Glad to oblige. You do look a little better this afternoon. Not so pale."

"I feel better. Still weak, as you pointed out when threatening to handcuff and arrest me." She paused for a smile and was rewarded with his in return. Her stomach executed a tingly jitterbug. "I napped a long time, which helped, but when I awoke, the distant drumming was growing louder."

"So, you thought the medicine could stop the headache before it got crazy?"

"Exactly." She opened the pill bottle and downed one tablet with a sip of soup. "Mm. This soup is really good."

"The sandwich shop makes it fresh from scratch daily. A bachelor sheriff knows where to find the good stuff."

"No Mrs. Sheriff at home?"

"I'm too busy for a wife. She'd die of loneliness."

Not only a bachelor, but a confirmed, died in the wool bachelor without a thought of marriage. Good. She didn't like cops anyway. And she worried she could easily like this one too much.

She still had big plans for the future. True, they were stalled out at the moment, but once the trouble in Texas settled down, she'd start over. Somewhere.

"I have to get back to work."

"I'll see you in the morning?" Did she sound over-eager? "To get my car, I mean."

"Nearly forgot about that. I should have taken you while we were out."

"Tomorrow's fine. After the soup and the pain meds, I'll want to sleep anyway."

"First thing in the morning, I have to take my niece to enroll in school. She's staying with me for a while, but I can pick you up before then."

Dallas was a little disappointed. She'd planned to

invite him to lunch or breakfast after retrieving her car. To repay his kindness. Maybe it was a blessing, though. After the nightmare with Aaron, she didn't want to get involved.

Who was she kidding? She was disappointed because something she couldn't name vibrated between them every time Lawson came around. Something magic and thrilling.

Either that or the migraine had stolen her last brain cell.

Probably that.

"Anytime is fine," she said. "Shoot me a text. I'll be ready."

"I'll need your number." Nothing flirtatious in the request. Strictly business.

"Of course." She rattled it off while he typed it into his contacts.

"Got it." He put the cell phone away and patted his shirt pocket. "You take care now."

"I will. And thank you again."

The handsome sheriff hesitated as if he wanted to say more, then nodded and left. The heavy hotel door clanged shut behind him.

MADISON DID NOT WANT to cooperate.

"School stinks. Kids hate me." She sat on the couch, arms folded, hair like something out of a brush pile.

Lawson stood in front of her, hands on his hips. "They won't if you'll lose the attitude and show them some consideration. Calypso is filled with good people."

Madison rolled her eyes. She was an expert at that. "Not *too* good, Sherlock, or they wouldn't need cops."

He wasn't going to argue. As he did with belligerent citizens, he demanded. "Get up. Get your clothes on, your hair combed. We leave in fifteen minutes."

To keep his cool, he went out to check on the horses. Sadie, an aging buckskin mare, stayed close to the barn and to her barn buddy, Tripp, a sweet palomino gelding. Lawson pampered them with extra feed and a rub down. After breaking a few blocks of hay and filling the water trough, he was sufficiently calm to return to the house.

Madison stood in the middle of the living room, the backpack on her shoulder. She looked presentable.

"Ready?"

"I guess."

With an inward sigh, he led the way to the car. Madison's attitude had to change. The problem was, short of handcuffing her and tossing her in juvie, he didn't know how to break through the wall she'd built around herself. She had issues. But who didn't?

"Gotta stop by the hotel first."

"Why?" She slammed inside and put on her seatbelt. "Someone get robbed?"

"The sick woman I told you about needs a ride to her car." Not that she couldn't walk or call the one taxi in town, but he'd offered, she'd accepted, and he wasn't complaining. She intrigued him.

Yes, it was unusual for him to do pick-up and delivery for anyone other prisoners, but he considered this a community service. Made the town seem friendly.

When they arrived at the hotel, Dallas came out as if she'd been watching for them. Lawson's stomach took a nose dive. The gorgeous blonde no longer appeared ill and wan. She looked high class. Way too high class for him. And pretty enough to be on TV. Leggy and slender with the posture perfect walk of a model.

Lawson shook his head to clear it. He wasn't in the market for romance. Not this week anyway. He had his hands full with his niece.

Nevertheless, he got out of the SUV and opened the back door for Dallas. "Sorry about the wire cage."

She stooped low and slid onto the backseat, then looked up at him. "I have to admit, this is my first ride in the backseat of a police car."

"Good to know." He leaned in, hands on either side of the door. "Though I do owe you a speeding ticket."

"Seriously?"

She looked so shocked, he allowed the inward smile to bloom on his lips. "Sixty in a thirty-five the day I found you defacing our pristine sidewalk."

She scrunched up her face—and looked mighty cute doing it. "Will an apology help?"

Another of those smiles might. "Possibly."

"How about an offer to buy your dinner?"

Was she flirting? "Sounds like bribing an officer of the court to me, doesn't it to you, Madison?"

Madison had turned in the seat and listened to the conversation with open curiosity. "Depends on how good the dinner is."

The unexpected levity brought a bark of laughter. The kid had a sense of humor?

Dallas grinned. "Your niece is brilliant. And she's invited to dinner, too. I promise it'll be good—if you recommend the restaurant." She leaned toward the mesh wire separating the backseat from the front. "I'm Dallas."

"I'm Madison." The teen managed to look surly, as if she hated her name.

"Ah. The sheriff's niece who's enrolling in school today."

"He told you about me?"

"Yes, but he forgot to mention how pretty you are."

Madison turned two shades of pink. "Thanks."

"First day in a new place is uncomfortable. Are you nervous?"

Lawson left them talking, closed the door and returned to the driver's side. When he got in, they were still talking, though some of Madison's snarky replies made him wince. Hadn't Bryce taught her anything?

When they arrived at Dallas's car, he had to get out and open her door. Backdoors were prisoner proof and didn't open from the inside.

Lawson offered a hand. Not because he wanted to touch her, though that was a nice bonus. But the seat was scooped so low, she needed the lift or she'd have to crawl out on hands and knees. Another intentional means of subduing prisoners.

Dallas got out, and they stood close in the open

door, the wind swirling around their feet. Her expensive fragrance teased his senses.

Lawson cleared his throat. "About that dinner. I'm free tonight."

"Rain check, maybe? I can't tonight." She fidgeted, glanced away. "I have an important phone call to make."

What did a phone call have to do with dinner, which, after all, had been her idea in the first place? An idea he'd latched onto like a snapping turtle.

"Right. I understand." A brush off was a brush off.

"I don't think you do, and I can't explain yet." Her blue eyes were troubled. "I may need your advice."

"Advice is free. You have my card." He stepped to the side and waited until she entered her Equinox and started the engine. As she backed out, she waved.

And a disappointed Lawson figured that would be the last time he'd see Dallas Langley.

CHAPTER 4

The headache was gone. She felt fine except for the nervous trembling in the pit of her stomach.

Dallas stared at her cell phone as if willing it to initiate the call to Wyatt Caldwell's number. If she called, he'd want to meet, which had been the whole purpose of her trip to Calypso, but now that she was here, she was scared.

What would he think of her? Would she be resented? Rejected? A disappointment? Would he know about the incident back in Bayville?

He must have some kind of evidence leading him to believe they were siblings. After all, he'd tracked her down. He knew things about her. She knew nothing about him or his family.

What if they were awful? Lowlifes, or worse, criminals? What if they wanted to extort money from her? What if she'd inherited something, and they wanted to lure her here and kill her rather than give it up?

She pressed fingers to each temple. "Stop. Just stop. You're letting your imagination go wild."

To prove as much, she sucked in a breath and pressed the number. The *brrr* continued for several moments and then, "Hello."

It was him, Wyatt. She recognized the voice. "Mr. Caldwell, this is Dallas Langley. I've been thinking about your invitation, and I'm in Calypso."

"That's great. When can we meet?" He sounded exceptionally eager.

"This is rather an awkward situation. I'm not sure of the best plan."

"We're all out of our element on this, Dallas." His deep voice was kind.

"We?"

"You, me, my family. You'll get to meet them, too, if you're willing."

He said the last with a hint of question, as if he wasn't certain of her wishes. She wasn't either.

"I'd prefer to meet only with you at first, if that's all right?"

"Whatever works for you. Name the time and place."

The offer made her feel more in control. She could do this. Maybe.

"I'm staying at the Best Western. Perhaps the hotel lobby?" A nice, safe, public place that offered enough privacy for a conversation but not enough for murder.

"Okay. When's a good time?"

"Tomorrow? Perhaps two o'clock?" The extra day gave her plenty of time to leave town if she changed her mind.

"Two tomorrow. I'll be there."

"Mr. Caldwell," she hurried to say, fearing he was about to hang up. "Does anyone else know about... our relationship?"

"Only the family at the moment. We want to respect your privacy. Anything more is your call."

"I appreciate the thoughtfulness. This has come as quite a shock to me."

"To us, too. You must have a lot of questions."

"Tons."

"I don't have all the answers, but I have some. Along with some questions of my own."

"Including proof of your...claims?"

"Yes, ma'am. DNA is quite conclusive. You are definitely my half-sister."

DNA. *Oh.* She'd taken one of those online tests on a lark more than a year ago but never checked for matches, afraid of discovering her birth father was a serial murderer or something equally as heinous. The possibility of siblings had never crossed her mind.

"Tomorrow, then," she said, "at two."

"See you then." The line went dead, and Dallas tumbled backwards across the bed and lay there staring at the hotel sprinkler head.

Maybe the time had come to ask someone about the Caldwell family.

And Dallas knew exactly who to call.

"SHERIFF, you're never going to believe this."

Lawson scribbled his name at the bottom of a report before looking up at Deputy Ronnie Shell. Lawson had been in rural law enforcement long enough to believe anything.

"Believe what?"

"I made a DUI arrest this morning."

Nothing unusual about that, unfortunately. "Someone started pretty early."

"Well, you see, Sheriff, it was Miss Pearly Wilson."

"Miss Pearly?" Lawson knew the elderly woman enjoyed a hot toddy in cold weather—she'd offered him one a couple of times when he'd stopped in to do a security check, but DUI? "When did she get a car?"

"She didn't." The deputy waited, enjoying the telling too much to hurry. "She was riding a horse. Right down highway 62. And singing the *Star Spangled Banner* at the top of her voice while waving an American flag."

Lawson laughed. He couldn't help it. The thought of the scrawny old lady doing such a thing was too ridiculous not to.

"And you arrested her?"

"Yes, sir. I had to before a car hit her. She offered me a sip from her flask."

Lawson shook his head. "Where is she now?"

"In holding, sleeping it off. Jeff Benson put the horse in his pasture for now."

Lawson went to the coffee pot atop the filing cabinet for another cup. His office was small, mostly a desk and file cabinets with a bulletin board loaded with wanted posters.

"Take her home as soon as she's sober and safe.

Give her daughter a call, too. If Joan's not available, make a safety check before nightfall." As much as the incident tickled his funny bone, Lawson would rather be safe than sorry.

Deputy Shell left the office, and Lawson returned to his desk, pulling out another incident form. The vandalism at the cemetery burned in his mind. Such reckless disrespect got his back up.

A peck at the door drew his attention. He sighed. A mountain of paperwork rested on his desk. Some peace and quiet without interruptions would be nice.

Tempted to yell, "Go away," he squinted through the rain glass in his office door but couldn't see a thing.

"Come on in." His tone was about as aggravated as he felt.

The door eased open. A blond head poked around the edge. "Did I choose a bad time?"

Lawson's gut lurched. Dallas Langley. Forget the paperwork. He stood. "Didn't mean to yell at you. Come on in."

"You're busy."

"Always, so don't worry about that." He motioned toward a chair across from his desk. "Sit. What can I do for you?"

She sat, and so did he, though his mind tumbled with questions and his veins buzzed with renewed energy. She was only in Calypso temporarily but that didn't mean he couldn't enjoy her company for now.

"Did you get your niece enrolled in school?" she asked, as if she were genuinely interested.

"I did. She wasn't excited, but the principal called in another student to show her the ropes today. Hopefully, that'll help."

"Being the new kid's tough."

"Her attitude doesn't help matters. But you impressed her. She thought you were cool." He didn't add the rest, that Madison had asked if Dallas was his girlfriend. "But you didn't come to ask about my niece. What can I do for you?"

"I need some information. But before I ask, I'd like your assurance that our conversation won't leave this room."

"All right. As long as it's legal."

"It is." She fiddled with the clasp on a pink clutch purse. Sparkly rhinestones glittered under the fluorescent lights. "I'm in town to meet some people I don't know. I want to be sure it's safe to do so."

Lawson folded his hands on the desktop and

leaned toward her. "Are you asking me to a run a background check?"

"Nothing like that." And then more eagerly, "Would you?"

He chuckled. "Why don't we start with what I know? Do you have a name?"

He could think of dozens of unsavory characters around the county. Hopefully, she wasn't hooked up with any of them.

"Caldwell. The man I spoke to was Wyatt Caldwell."

Lawson sat back, hiding a smile. "Bad hombre, that Wyatt."

Dallas leaned forward, eyes wide. "Seriously?"

He laughed. "Not serious at all. Wyatt Caldwell is a great guy, a good friend of mine, as is the entire Caldwell clan. If you have business dealings with them, you can count on a fair deal with Christian people who'll treat you like family."

She winced and lost her smile. "That's the other thing."

"What other thing?"

"Mr. Caldwell believes we're related. Closely. As in, I'm his half-sister."

Lawson felt his mouth dropped open. He, a law dog who'd seen and heard everything, was stunned.

"Do I resemble them at all?"

"Not a bit."

"Oh." She seemed disappointed. "Maybe he's mistaken. Things like that happen. This could be a wild goose chase."

"Which parent does he think you share?"

"A dad. I never knew mine, never even knew who he was, so the possibility is there."

"Clint Caldwell." Clint had been devoted to his late wife. He didn't fit the stereotype of philanderers, and he sure wasn't the kind of man who would abandon his child.

"Is that his name? My…possible father?"

"You really don't know anything about them, do you?"

"No, I got the completely unexpected call from Wyatt the day I came here."

"And ended up in our fine medical facility."

"Right. When Wyatt first called, I'd already had a stressful day, so I didn't ask many questions. I think I've been too stunned, and I haven't had time to do any investigating on my own. I suppose I could have Googled them." She gazed down at her lap, her fingers fiddling nervously with her wallet clasp. "I can't believe this is really happening. Can't believe someone would call me out of the blue and claim to be my brother. It's weird and scary."

"But you drove here as soon as you got the call. Wyatt must have said something to convince you."

"Truth is, I'd just gotten fired from my job and…" She glanced away, pulled her bottom lip between her teeth, let it go. Oh, it was a lush and lovely lip. So was the top one, kissed with the faintest blush of color. "I needed to get out of town for a few days. Get my head together and make some decisions. Calypso was a good excuse."

"And yet, your head came apart."

She laughed softly, titling that pretty head. "That's certainly the way it felt."

He rubbed a hand down his shirt front, felt the thud of his heart. Dallas was easy to talk to, pretty to look at, had a sense of humor. And was way out of his league. Probably a fashion model in Dallas or an executive in some very smart firm. And he was a small-town sheriff with cowboy in his blood.

"What did you do back in Bayville?" He knew she was from the Dallas suburb. Perks of being a law dog.

She hesitated long enough to raise his curiosity and make him wonder why she hadn't wanted to answer. "I hosted a radio program. Medium market, but a great start. Tunes and talk with some of the sweetest callers." Sadness crossed her features.

"You miss it."

"And you're very observant."

Lawson tapped his badge. Dallas smiled. And he got a light, airy feeling in his chest.

Ridiculous. He appreciated a pretty face as much as any red-blooded American male, and he'd had his share of propositions, particularly from law-breakers. But he'd just met this woman. How could he be this attracted so soon?

"I loved my work," she was saying, "and even though it's only been a few days, I miss it terribly."

"I'd bet you were good." Considering the quality of her voice, warm, velvety, low enough to be sensual without being suggestive, she'd attract people like an ice cream truck at summer camp.

"I *am* good. And I'm determined to get back in the business very soon." She shifted, straightening. "But right now, my focus is on meeting the Caldwells."

He picked up a pen and tapped it on his desk calendar. "I'd be happy to introduce you."

Dallas gave her head a negative shake. Lawson shouldn't have been disappointed, but he was.

"I appreciate that, Sheriff, but Wyatt and I are

meeting tomorrow afternoon in the hotel lobby. Now that I know he's a solid human being and not some maniac who found my phone number on the internet."

"Actually, he probably did. He's a computer expert for the army. But he's not a maniac. That would be his oldest brother." When she looked up with a shocked expression, he lifted a hand. "Joking. You're in good hands. And don't be surprised if they invite you to dinner at the ranch. If they do, smile and agree. You won't regret it. Connie is the best cook in Calypso County."

"Connie?"

"She's the Caldwell's…" Lawson pressed a finger to his upper lip. "Hmm, how to describe Connie. She's their cook and housekeeper, but she's a lot more. She raised the Caldwell kids after their mom died. They consider her part of the family. We all do."

"That's good to know. Thank you. You've made this easier." Manicured hands smoothed the sides of her long, pink sweater. A calming technique, Lawson recognized. He was good with body language. Had to be in his line of business. He waited her out. Let her talk. The fact that he liked hearing her smooth voice was a bonus.

"Now that I know I'll be in a town a few days," she said, "let's talk about that dinner I owe you."

"You don't owe me anything."

"Then consider it a dinner between new friends. Turns out I'm available tonight after all. How about around six-thirty? The Roadhouse Turf and Surf?"

"My favorite restaurant. How did you know?"

She shrugged, a graceful lift of shoulders. "Except for the fact that I asked the hotel desk clerk for recommendations, I never knew a man to resist a big, juicy steak with all the trimmings."

"Certainly, not this man. But I'm buying."

"No way! I invited you."

"You're unemployed."

She pretended insult. "Thanks for that painful reminder."

Lawson laughed. She joined him.

And suddenly he was looking very forward to tonight.

WALKING into a restaurant with the local sheriff was like being on the arm of a celebrity. Even the wait staff greeted him by name, though he'd left his uniform behind and wore dark blue jeans, cowboy boots, and a blue button-down that only added to his appeal. The black leather bomber jacket didn't hurt either. He was definitely easy on the eyes, as every female in the place seemed to notice.

If Dallas had known him longer, she might be jealous. As it was, she felt a certain element of pride being the woman on his arm. Now, how silly was that? A career-minded woman running away from a relationship that ended in the worst possible way shouldn't even consider getting involved again.

But a dinner didn't mean involvement. Right now, she was looking for a distraction. Between the Caldwells and Lawson, she'd found plenty.

"The scent in here is divine," she said.

"Nothing like steaks sizzling on the grill." He touched the small of her back, guiding her through the maze of customers and waiters to a booth near the back. She liked that, too, the courteous way he treated her, the light touch of a warm, masculine hand. "Their lobster is good, too, if you'd rather."

"Steak sounds fabulous. My appetite returned with a vengeance this afternoon."

He politely held her coat while she slid it off, and then removed his jacket so that she had a pleasant view of his fit chest and shoulders. A man didn't get this honed sitting behind a desk or riding in a police car.

The buzz of attraction grew louder in her ears.

Or else, the migraine was coming back.

Her lips curved at the silly thought. The good-looking sheriff and a migraine headache were too very different things.

She slid into the booth across from Lawson and took the menu offered by the waiter.

"I'm Kenny," the red-haired waiter said. "I'll be your server tonight. Would you like to start your meal off with wine or beer?"

"Not for me." Lawson said. "Sweet tea's good."

Kenny was young, probably a college student. He scribbled on his pad. "I knew you'd say that, Sheriff. How about for the lady?"

"Tea for me, as well." Dallas smiled up at the waiter. "Unsweetened with lemon."

After the waiter left, she folded her arms along the table edge. It seemed odd to feel this relaxed with a man she barely knew.

"Wyatt called me shortly before you arrived at the hotel."

"Any new developments?"

"He sent some documents to my email, but I only gave them a glance. I don't like reading on my phone screen."

"You could use my computer. I have a laptop at home."

"That's a thoughtful offer. Thank you."

"After dinner, we can drive out to my ranch if you'd like."

She tilted her head, realized she was flirting. "Why, Sheriff Hawk, are you offering to show me the proverbial etchings?"

He laughed. "Not with a surly thirteen-year-old in residence."

"Why didn't she come with you tonight?"

"Refused. Said she didn't want to sit around and watch a couple of old people stare at each other and talk about stupid, boring stuff." His lips quirked. "Her words, unfortunately, and her general attitude. She probably had too much homework."

"Has she lived with you very long?" She couldn't imagine a law-and-order cop tolerating that kind of bad behavior. Her stepdads certainly hadn't.

"Arrived a few days ago. Unexpectedly." One of his eyebrows twitched, expression serious. There was a story there. If she'd been on air, she would have pried a little. Maybe she would anyway.

"She's defensive, isn't she?" She'd noticed an edge, a chip, this morning when talking to Madison, and as a professional listener, she'd felt the undercurrents in the girl's comments. Madison wasn't a happy child.

"Defensive. Belligerent. Resentful." He blew out a sigh. "I don't know what to do about it. Taking on a teenage girl, even short term, is outside my wheelhouse."

"Give you an armed robber or a drug runner any day, huh?" she asked lightly.

His lips curved. "*Any* day. I know what to do with them."

Dallas put down the spoon, interested. The girl had tweaked her sympathy, and so had the man. Especially the man. And offering advice was one of the things she did best. At least on the radio.

The waiter returned with their drinks, took their orders, and left again. The restaurant hummed with activity, but Dallas barely noticed. Lawson Hawk had her full attention.

He had an ease about him that drew her, as if they'd known each other far longer than a few days.

"Girls that age are going through a lot of crazy emotions," she said, "most of which they don't understand. Did she want to come for this visit? Or was that someone else's idea?"

"Her dad's choice, without my permission."

"Wow. That says a lot." She folded her hands on

the tabletop. "What did he do? Just drop her off at the mailbox and drive away?"

"Worse. He took off to Nashville to be a star, and she hitchhiked to my place."

Dallas sucked in a gasp. "Unbelievable."

"Isn't it? But that's my irresponsible half brother."

"Poor Madison. Talk about rejection. Hitch-hiking is so scary."

"And I don't suppose I've helped. I'm a busy, single guy." He spread his hands, palms up. "Never much interested in kids. I don't know what to do with her."

She used her best *Dallas after Dark* voice—kind, but gently probing. "She probably feels your reluctance, Lawson, and feels equally horrible because being here is out of her control. She didn't want to come. You didn't want her here."

He rotated his tea glass and exhaled, a heavy breath. "I sound like a jerk."

"A jerk wouldn't be concerned."

"I suppose." He sipped his tea, pondered. "I don't really know her, but I care about her, and I want her to be happy. So far, all I do is make her angry."

"More defenses. Could she be afraid if she lets down her guard, she'll like you or get attached? And caring might bring her more rejection?"

Their food arrived, steam wafting up from the steaks and loaded baked potatoes. They took a few seconds to organize their table and dab sauce on their KC Strips. The waiter brought fragrant yeast rolls and refilled glasses.

When he'd left, Lawson cut into his steak and said, "You're good at this psychology stuff, you know that?"

"Tricks of the trade." When he tilted his head, questioning, she went on. "My radio show is a mix of music and advice and friendly conversation. I started out as a host on the morning drive show, but my bosses quickly realized I had a knack for getting listeners to open up and talk, which led to more call-ins and listeners."

"And your own special show?"

"Dallas after Dark." As soon as she spoke, Dallas wanted the words back. Lawson might look the show up online, which would lead him to the situation she was trying to get away from.

She guided the conversation back to safe ground. "Does Madison have an aunt or grandma nearby? Another female to talk with might help her."

"No one. Poor kid. She's stuck with me, a crotchety old Uncle Sheriff."

Dallas's lips curved. Lawson Hawk was a charmer. She wondered if he even knew?

She sliced another portion of the succulent meat and let the scent fill her nostrils. "This steak is delicious. Tender, perfectly cooked. No wonder you like to eat here."

With a half smile, Lawson saluted her with his fork. "Eat. Enjoy. Sorry to bore you with my personal problems. You have enough on your mind."

A truer statement than he knew. But for a few hours today, she'd had enough distractions to keep her from thinking about Aaron. She'd cared about him, at least in the beginning, and now, she ached for what had happened. But nothing she did was going to change the outcome.

Lawson touched her forearm. "Hey, where'd you go? Why so sad?"

She shook off the memory, intentionally brightening. The sheriff wouldn't be interested in her personal heartaches. He, too, had enough on his mind.

"Unintentional, I assure you. I'm thoroughly enjoying myself. And I don't mind talking about your niece. I like helping." It was who she was, what she did.

Except she hadn't been able to help Aaron.

CHAPTER 5

*L*awson hoped like crazy that Madison would behave herself.

His house lights were ablaze as he guided his beautiful date up the steps. He knocked. "It's me, Uncle Burglar. Let me in."

Beside him, Dallas snickered. "I hope Madison doesn't come to the door with an iron skillet in her hand."

He fumbled in his pocket for a key and found it just as Madison unlocked the door. She didn't even bother with a greeting. She gave him a why-are-you-bothering-me look, turned around and went back inside the house, disappearing down the hall a moment later.

Lawson exchanged a glance with Dallas. "Sorry."

"Don't worry about it." She entered the living room in front of him and placed her clutch and coat on the nearest chair back. She was comfortable in herself, and he liked that in a woman.

Fact was, he liked a lot of things about Dallas Langley. Other than being eye-burning pretty, she was smart, funny, warm and friendly, and extremely easy to talk to. She was also ambitious. A good thing, but also a good reason for him to keep a distance. Dallas was only visiting. Granted, if she and the Caldwells were family, the chances of him seeing her again were increased, but she was the type to make it big somewhere. Calypso was too small for a smart, gorgeous woman with big dreams.

Tell that to his heart. Tonight, when he'd picked her up at the hotel, his pulse had raced to see her walking toward him across the lobby. She'd looked elegant in short, high-heeled boots and a long, black dress slit up to her knee, her sleek hair gleaming against a hot pick cardigan.

He was out of his league but enjoying the ride while it lasted.

"Would you like some coffee?" He motioned toward the kitchen. "Fast and easy in the Keurig."

"Nothing for me, thanks. I'm stuffed from that

wonderful dinner." She remained in the living room, taking in his comfy black sofa and chair, the television that spanned one wall and was definitely too big for the room, the mish-mash of end tables he'd bought at a ranch auction because he'd liked them. Rustic barn wood with wrought iron corner braces on top and black, metal-worked cowboys around the bottom.

Lawson was glad he kept the place in decent shape. But if Dallas saw his closet, she'd faint. Not that she'd have any reason to look inside his closet.

"Have a seat, and I'll grab my laptop from the bedroom." He left her in the living room and passed down the hall, not bothering to stop until he reached Madison's room.

The door stood open. She was sprawled across the end of the bed, scribbling in her journal. He pecked a knuckle against the wood.

Madison looked up, frowning. "Why do you keep knocking?"

"Because knocking is considered good manners, and so is greeting a guest."

"Why? She's not interested in me. Her eyes are all over you."

As much as he liked the sound of that, Lawson said, "Why not go in and at least say hello?"

"Dad always told me to make myself scarce when he brought home women."

Your dad needs a swift kick. "I'm not your dad."

"Ain't that the truth?" She closed the journal and sauntered past him.

He called behind her. "There's a carry-out container on the table if you're hungry."

She whipped around. "You brought me carry-out?"

Again, that incredulous expression that said she was accustomed to fending for herself. "I hope steak is all right."

"It'll do." For a moment, the girl stood in the dimly lit hallway, one hip lower than the other. Then, she whipped around and started toward the living room. "I *love* steak."

The words were barely uttered, but Lawson heard them.

Dallas's idea. Brilliant woman.

He retrieved the laptop from the bedroom where he'd worked last night on a sheriff's never-ending paperwork. He'd rather spend his days among the people of the county than at his desk, so a lot of paperwork followed him home.

Before he could leave the room, his cell phone

buzzed. As eager as he was to get back to his date, he had an obligation to answer.

It was the sheriff in the next county, updating him on a meeting scheduled for next week, asking him to present a report on drug traffic through the area. After a couple of minutes, they rang off.

"Here you go." He re-entered the living room to find Dallas sitting on the ottoman in front of his favorite chair. Madison was in it.

They were talking about fashion. Something about booties versus boots and what clothes to wear with which style.

He tried not to make a face.

Dallas looked up at him and smiled. "We're discussing the merits of boots."

"Scintillating information, I'm sure."

She laughed. "It is to us girls."

"And you know what?" Madison leaned up, surprisingly animated. "Dallas and I wear the same size!"

"Shocking."

It was the wrong response. Madison lost her sparkle and flopped back against the chair. He'd been teasing. But she must have taken his remark as condescension.

Dallas came to his rescue. She bent toward her

boot and took hold of the zipper. "Want to try these on?"

"Can I?"

"You may."

The exchange was made, and Madison gushed like the teen she was.

The boot was one of those ankle styles with sharp heels that made Dallas almost as tall as him. Not very practical on a ranch, but sexy as all get out. On Dallas. Madison was a tad awkward as she clomped and wobbled around the hardwood floor.

Dallas sat on his ottoman, knees crossed, swinging her bare foot, smiling at the young girl.

It was the first time he'd seen Madison show the slightest interest in anything.

"Wait, wait. We need a picture." Dallas snapped open her clutch and removed a cell phone.

"Okay." Madison sounded almost breathless. Didn't her dad snap pictures of her? Probably not. Did anyone?

"Strike a pose. Hand on hip. Toss your hair."

Madison followed the instructions, giggling, her face pink while Dallas took several photos.

"There we go."

"Can I see?" Madison scooched onto the ottoman

to remove the boots and look at photos. "I like that one."

"They're all good. You're photogenic."

"I am?"

"The proof's right here." Dallas held the phone toward him. "Isn't she, Lawson?"

All he saw was an awkward kid playing grown-up. But that was not an observation she'd want to hear. "Can you send that one to my cell?"

"Sure."

In a few taps, Lawson heard his phone ping.

For once, Madison actually looked happy. Thanks to Dallas. He almost hated to change the subject.

"Sorry to break up the fashion shoot, but Dallas needs to borrow my laptop for a few minutes."

"Right." The attitude was back. "I got stuff to do anyway." Madison tugged off the boots and handed them back to Dallas.

"You have food in the kitchen."

"Not hungry. You kids have fun." She disappeared down the hallway. Her bedroom door closed with a snap.

Lawson heaved a heavy sigh. One step forward and two leaps back.

.   .   .

DALLAS HEARD Madison's door close, but her focus was on the man standing in the middle of the living room, staring down the hall, looking about as lost as a man could look.

After replacing her boots, she rose from the ottoman and went to him. Compassion was one of her strengths, but it was also a weakness. She could never turn away from someone hurting. In this house, there were two hurting souls.

"Hey." She put a hand on his arm. It was rock hard, tense, like his jaw.

He gave his head a little shake and turned toward her. "See what I mean? I upset her, but I have no clue what I did."

Her compassion shot a little higher. Along with the thought that Lawson was a good man. And she didn't like thinking of cops as good guys. "Want me to talk to her?"

"Nah. Won't do any good." He rubbed the back of his neck, brow furrowed. "Would you mind?"

"Talking's what I do," she said softly, wondering why she still held his arm, and why she still stood close enough to see the black ring around his gorgeous irises. "Do you mind if she eats in her room?"

"I'd rather she didn't get into the habit, but maybe this once, if you think it would help."

"Never mind. I'll use the food as a lure." She winked and started down the hall.

"I'll boot up the computer."

She looked over one shoulder, saw the cowboy sheriff moving toward the center island and the laptop he'd brought in. Something far stronger than a flutter moved through her.

Stop it. Just stop it, she told herself. *Look, but don't touch. Enjoy, but don't get involved.* Especially now, not after Aaron and not with the Caldwell issue hanging in limbo.

At the moment, she didn't even know who she was.

As Dallas walked the short hall with four doors leading off to the left and right, she realized she hadn't asked which room was Madison's. She pecked on the first one, peeked inside, and found a bathroom. The next room contained a weight set and a treadmill. No wonder the sheriff was fit and trim.

She closed the door, moved to the next where she tapped again and opened. This had to be Lawson's room. It screamed him in all his masculine, cowboy glory.

A brown comforter with blue southwest designs

around the edge covered a big bed made of dark, sturdy wood. A star was carved into the headboard. A tall chest and night stand matched the bed, complete with smaller stars. A photo of a man and boy sat on the nightstand, and a gorgeous painting of running horses hung on one wall.

She inhaled, holding her breath to keep the masculine scent inside in her head. The room even smelled like him, and, except for Lawson's black bomber jacket tossed across the bed, was neat and clean. Her perfectionist tendencies were pleased.

Dallas caught herself, realized she was prying, and quickly shut the door and moved on. She pecked on the last door and received no answer, but by process of elimination, she knew this had to be Madison's room.

She turned the knob. Locked. She leaned closer. "Madison. It's Dallas. Can we talk? Please."

After a long moment of rustling sounds, the knob wobbled and the door opened. Dallas's heart squeezed. The girl's eyes were red.

"Oh, honey."

"I'm not crying. I have sinus issues."

"Which you weren't experiencing five minutes ago."

Madison cocked one hip, eyebrows up, lip curled. "So?"

"So, I care. Your uncle cares. We want to help."

The tough expression wobbled. Just a little, but enough that Dallas knew she was making progress. "Come on. Let's sit and talk for a minute."

"Won't my uncle get cold without you to snuggle up with?"

"Your uncle and I are only friends. New friends, at that."

"Never slowed my dad down."

Your dad is a... a word I don't want to think. "I'd like to be your friend, too."

"Why?"

"Because I think you need one, and so do I."

Madison flopped onto the bed's edge, head leaned back as if the ceiling were her best friend.

"My old man doesn't want me. Uncle Lawson doesn't want me. My mom ran off because I'm such a wonderful kid. I don't expect you to stick around either."

"Friends don't have to be in the same town to be friends. I'm only visiting here, but we can talk on the phone, text, social media."

Madison brought her head down and squinted. "You do social media? Like Snapchat and stuff?"

"I do." Though when Aaron had begun his craziness, she'd set all her accounts to private. Neither that, nor a restraining order, had stopped him. "I haven't been online in a while. Things going on in my life. But—"

"What kind of things?" Leave it to a teenager to latch onto that part of the conversation.

No way was she discussing Aaron with anyone, certainly not a thirteen-year-old. "It's hard to talk about."

"I know what you mean."

Dallas sat down on the edge of the bed, angling to face Madison. "I think you do, so I'll tell you." A little. "I lost my job."

"That's tough. What kind of job? Were you a model or something?"

She gave a short laugh. "No, but thank you for the compliment. I had my own show on the radio."

"No way! Get out of here! That is the coolest thing ever!"

If she'd known the word radio would bring out the exclamations, she'd have tossed it out sooner.

"I loved my work. Still love it and plan to find another job in radio as soon as...I can." As soon as the stench of her terrible failure stopped making the rounds of the radio world.

"So how long are you staying here? In Calypso, I mean?"

"I haven't decided yet."

"I hope it's a long time. Maybe you could even work for the station here in town. I know there is one, because we drive past it on the way to school."

"I'll keep that in mind." Starting over? In a small market? Not if she could help it. "Your uncle drives you to school? That's nice of him."

"I guess. Riding in a cop car is weird, and everybody stares, but it beats riding the stinky bus."

"I'd feel the same," Dallas said. "How was school?"

"Other than the fact that I hate it, hate my teachers, hate the dumb kids in my class, I guess it's okay. I made a B on an English test today, and I wasn't even here for the whole unit."

"Which means you're a smart cookie. Speaking of cookies, reminds me of food. Yours." Dallas stood, tugging the girl up with her. "Let's go feed you. That steak smells amazing."

"Won't I be in the way?"

"Not at all. I want you in there."

"For real? Or are you blowing smoke?"

"No smoking allowed."

Madison rolled her eyes at the pun, but she laughed too. "Okay."

They started out of the room. As they traversed the hall, Madison paused to ask, "Sometime, when you have time. I mean, not now. That's too much trouble. And you're really busy."

Dallas touched the girl's shoulder. "Just ask."

"Will you show me how you make your eyebrows look like that, all clean and perfect?"

"Sure. If it's okay with your uncle."

"He's not my boss."

"Actually, he is, Madison. And he's not a bad guy. Give him a break."

"Yeah, whatever."

They came into the living room, and Madison headed around the center island toward the kitchen and her food.

Lawson stood on the living-area side of the island, sipping a cup of coffee. He raised one eyebrow at Dallas in question. She gave a silent nod and a smile, and he looked so relieved, she wanted to hug him.

Silly thought. So, to keep her arms to herself, she moved to the computer he'd set up on the island and climbed onto a bar stool.

"Did Madison tell you about her English test? She made a B. And she wasn't even here to study the unit."

"Seriously?" To his credit, he leaned across the island and said, "Good going, Madison."

The teen was too busy stuffing down steak and loaded baked potato to answer, but her cheeks reddened and her eyes sparkled.

Lawson shot Dallas a grateful look and mouthed, "Thanks."

She hadn't really done anything except talk to the child. But then, talking was her gift.

Dallas logged into her email. Sure enough, there was the message from Wyatt Caldwell. She didn't open it.

She shook out her hands, wiggled her fingers. "I'm nervous."

Lawson scooted a bar stool up close to hers so that their shoulders brushed. "Need company, or want to do this alone? I can make myself scarce."

His voice was low, almost tender, and altogether masculine.

A quiver of awareness moved through her again. She swallowed, nervous for a brand-new reason. *Him.* "Company. But just...sit here. Don't read anything."

He squeezed the top of her hand where it lay on the island granite. "Deal."

He shifted slightly, his eyes on her instead of the

computer. Which only made her more of aware of him.

His cologne, some warm, musky fragrance that reminded her of the woods in summer, swirled around her, light, barely there, but enough to be captivating.

And oh, my, she was starting to get out of control.

Madison's voice jerked her to her senses.

"Can I take this in my room?" She held up the carry out box.

She sounded almost like a normal, respectful kid.

"I'd rather you eat at the table," Lawson said.

"But I've got a math paper to finish, and I'm starving."

"All right. This once. But we're not making a habit of it."

She rolled her eyes. "I won't get steak sauce on your precious bedding or whatever you're having a cow about."

The teen scooted around them and left the room. Lawson got that helpless look again.

Dallas patted his forearm. "Stop worrying. You've made progress."

"How so?"

"She actually *asked* if she could take the food to her room. She didn't stomp away."

"That's true." He brightened.

Dallas clicked on the email, read it, and then clicked on the attachments, perusing each one in turn. When she'd finished, she minimized the entire email and sat back.

"He told me a little about the Caldwell family. Three brothers and a sister. Besides me." She licked dry lips. "The documents Wyatt attached are samples of my DNA compared to every single sibling."

"And," he gently urged.

"I know very little about DNA, but this looks legit." She nodded toward the computer.

"So, you are?"

"Yes. I think I am." She took a deep breath, tried to still the rattling in her bones, and said, "Though I can't wrap my head around it, it must be true. I'm their half-sister."

"You're shaking." He swiveled the chair around and pulled her hands into his lap, rubbing a thumb along the tops. "Are you okay? Not going to faint on me again, are you?"

His lips curved the slightest bit, and he looked so concerned and tender she nearly melted.

Must be the shock.

"No. I'm just...overwhelmed. A little scared. Shaken, really."

"You've never looked for your birth father?"

"Other than taking one of those online DNA tests, no. My mom says zero about her past life. I asked her a few times, and she got really upset. She always said she'd take it to her grave."

"I wonder why?"

"Isn't that obvious? My father has other kids. He was a married man. He and my mother had an affair, and I was a nasty little surprise."

He squeezed her hands. "Bet your mother didn't feel that way."

She shook her head. "She didn't. Even if she made terrible choices in men, including my father and the two husbands that are long gone, she loved me, spoiled me like a princess. I had a good childhood." Except for the times Mom was married.

"You're her only child? No siblings?"

She nudged her chin toward the computer. "Only these I've never met."

"The Caldwells are great people. If I had to pick a family, I'd pick them."

"You wouldn't choose your own?"

"Mine?" He gave a short laugh but didn't answer

DALLAS AND THE COWBOY

the question directly. "Just me and my dad. We did okay. My parents divorced when I was small."

"And then your mother married Madison's dad's father?"

"I can barely comprehend what you just said."

She laughed. He was making her feel better, calming her jitters. Nice guy, she thought again. How could he be a cop?

HE WAS GOING to regret this in the morning.

It was long past midnight, and Lawson still wasn't ready to say goodnight to Dallas.

As he walked her across the parking lot toward the hotel entrance, the moon lit a pathway and a cold wind circled them. He didn't resist the urge to tug her a bit closer to his side. Her long, elegant black coat was probably warm enough, but he ignored that fact. Smelling her perfume, feeling her hand enclosed inside his, listening to that velvety voice of hers, was mighty nice.

"You feel okay about seeing Wyatt tomorrow?"

"I do now. Thanks to you."

"If you need me…" He let the words dangle as they reached the hotel door and he opened it into the well-lit lobby. Warmth rushed toward them.

Out of courtesy for the other guests, they quieted then, regrettably, though they'd talked so much tonight he marveled that he had more to say to her.

The carpeted hallway was hushed beneath their feet. Even her heels were silent. At Room 5, she took her key from her clutch and turned to face him.

"I enjoyed tonight," she said.

"Me, too." He stared down into her eyes, feeling...*something*. "Maybe we can do it again."

"I'd like that."

"Tomorrow night? My place?" Did he sound too desperate? "I'm a serviceable cook."

"Sounds tempting." She pretended to consider. "I just happen to have tomorrow night open."

And the next, he hoped.

"After dinner, we could have a look at those etchings." He smiled to let her know he teased.

"Etchings are tempting, but I'd rather see your horses." She playfully batted her eyelashes and smiled. "For now."

If that didn't set his heart racing, he was dead.

"You like horses?"

"Very much. My mother was a barrel racer."

"Seriously?" This got better by the minute. "So, do you race, too?"

"I tried when I was younger, mostly to please her,

but I didn't have her fearless talent. I was better and happier in the press box."

"But you ride?"

"Oh, yes." She leaned her head to one side, her long hair swishing open to reveal big silver hoop earrings. "I owned a buckskin gelding until I moved to Bayville. Sweet boy."

Somehow he couldn't see Dallas as a horse woman. She looked too fancy, too into fashion and beauty to also be into horses. But the combination thrilled him to the toenails.

He thought about kissing her then. Her face was tilted up, eyes dancing, and she was close enough that all he'd have to do was lean in and press his mouth to hers.

But before he could, another guest entered the hall. He took a step back. He and Dallas exchanged regretful glances.

Some moments were too personal, too private to share with strangers. This was one of them. The county sheriff couldn't be caught in a hotel hallway kissing anyone, no matter how beautiful and agreeable she was.

But if he had any say in the matter, there would definitely be another time, another place.

CHAPTER 6

*D*allas paced the small hotel lobby, stopping every minute to peer through the large windows out into the parking lot. She wasn't sure what she was looking for. She didn't know what Wyatt Caldwell drove. She didn't even know what he looked like.

She wished she'd set the meeting up for morning instead of afternoon. Every minute that passed made her more nervous. And anxiety brought on the headaches. She pressed a finger tip to her temple. Nothing yet, thankfully.

Today's desk clerk was a matronly woman with short curly hair and a chain on her glasses. She kept giving Dallas curious looks. Nosey. But the lobby contained several small seating areas, and Dallas had chosen the one farthest from the desk. The last thing she wanted was for some total stranger to eavesdrop on the coming conversation. Wyatt probably felt the same.

She wiped moist palms down the side of her dress. Wanting to make a good first impression, she'd dressed nicely, as she would for a job interview, though the thought of looking for another job pained her. Blue-green enhanced her eye color, or so she'd been told, so she'd chosen a fitted turquoise dress and added a black jacket and the same black, high-heeled boots she'd worn to dinner with Lawson.

The thought of the sheriff and his niece brought a calming smile. He'd made her promise to call him after her conversation with Wyatt. Truth was, she was thrilled for the excuse to talk to the sheriff again.

Last night, he'd almost kissed her. There in the Best Western hallway, she'd absolutely tingled with anticipation. Then, he'd changed his mind and stepped away. Probably for the best. Getting involved with another man, especially a cop, wasn't on her agenda, but she'd been disappointed.

Now, here she was thinking about Lawson when

her whole life, or the life she'd known, was about to change.

Smoothing her skirt one more unnecessary time, Dallas wondered if she should have opted for something more casual. Too late now to change, and she hadn't brought an abundance of clothes on this impromptu trip to Calypso.

Her cell phone buzzed, and Dallas held her breath, hoping it wasn't her mother. She wasn't ready to tell Mom about this decision to meet the family she didn't know. Fact was, Mom didn't know about Wyatt's call. Dallas wanted to make sure everything was on the up and up before she opened what might be a painful Pandora's box to her mother.

One glance at the incoming text and her shoulders relaxed. It was Bethany, her best friend in Bayville.

Are you okay? Call me.

Bethany had no idea Dallas was in Calypso, but she knew about Aaron and understood how devastated Dallas was. First Aaron and then her job. Two losses back to back.

She moved her thumbs over the tiny keyboard. *About to have a meeting. Will call tonight. I'm okay. Have some crazy news.*

She hit *send* just as the outside door opened and a tall, sandy-haired man with impressive posture and an attractive, sculpted face strode in. He carried a laptop case.

Dallas's heart tumbled in her chest like a lottery barrel. Was this her brother?

They made eye contact, and the man came toward her, expression curious. "Dallas?"

She'd know that voice anywhere. "Yes. Are you Wyatt?"

"I am. Thank you for meeting me." He seemed intense, as if he was as anxious about this situation as she was. "Shall we sit?"

She motioned toward the farthest group of stuffed chairs. "More private back there." While still being close enough that she could scream for help if necessary. Not that she'd need to. Lawson had assured her the Caldwells were solid citizens, Christians even, and she trusted Lawson. Which was weird in and of itself.

Once they were seated, Wyatt took out his laptop and booted it up. "Did you get the documents I emailed to you?"

"Yes, and I read through them. Everything appears legitimate."

"It is, all of it carefully researched and vetted.

You're definitely our half-sister." He angled his square-jaw toward her, hazel eyes sincere. "So how do you feel about having a family you never knew existed?"

Her belly fluttered. The jury was still out on that one. "I could ask you the same, but I'd rather know about my father."

"*Our* father." He looked a little uncomfortable saying the words. She got that.

"I'm sorry," she said. "This is awkward for both of us."

She, who was normally glib of tongue and could squeeze conversation from a house plant, struggled for words.

"I hope we can get past that," he said.

"Do you?" Didn't he resent her and what she stood for even a little?

"Yes. We all do. All, meaning the family." He tapped a few keys on the screen and brought up a photo app. "I thought you might like to see some family pictures. Get acquainted."

"That was thoughtful. Lawson said you were a nice guy."

"You know Lawson Hawk?"

"We've met." And had dinner and sat up half the

night talking. And I have a skin-tingling crush on the man.

"I thought you'd never heard of Calypso."

She gave a little shoulder shrug. "He's the sheriff. I was speeding. We met."

"Ouch." Wyatt grimaced. "That's Lawson. Law and order all the way, even if the perp is gorgeous and related to his best friends."

She relaxed a little, glad for the lighter topic and the compliment, even if Wyatt was her brother. *Brother.* The term still made her head spin. She had brothers and a sister.

"To be completely honest, the sheriff rescued me. I was ill when I sped through Calypso. Lawson took me to the hospital."

The intense gaze grew fierce and protective. "You okay now? Anything serious? Is this meeting too much for you?"

She waved off the suggestion, though she appreciated his concern. "I suffer debilitating migraines on occasion. Nothing to worry about. I'm well now."

"Ace has those sometimes. My—our brother." He pointed at the computer screen. "That's him, the tallest one with the blackest hair. He and Emily—"he pointed to a pretty woman with a bright smile—"resemble our late mother. Black hair, green eyes, and stunning looks. The bulkier man in the cowboy hat is Nate, our other brother, the teddy-bear of the bunch. He looks more like Dad. This picture was taken at Christmas."

Dallas stared at the big family. To an only child, the number was overwhelming. "Who are the others?"

He pointed out wives and kids, his own lovely, blonde fiancé, a man in wheelchair, and a pair of employees he called family of the heart. "You'll meet them soon. I mean, if you're willing. You're invited to dinner any and every night you're in town, starting tonight."

"Oh, I can't tonight." The idea of meeting all those Caldwells at once scared her. Even if she hadn't been thrilled about seeing Lawson again, which she was, she'd have been glad for the excuse. "I already have other plans."

"Your decision. No pressure. But we want to know you, Dallas. Family is a big deal to the Caldwells. And you're a Caldwell."

"How can you consider me family? After all, my existence means..." She let the rest fade away, but the inference remained, and Wyatt was obviously a very intelligent man.

"None of us knows the circumstances of your

birth," he said, "but whatever it might be, we don't blame you, if that's what you're getting at."

Dallas gazed into his sincere eyes, puzzled that he could feel that way, but relieved as well. "It was. Thank you. This is difficult for me. I hope you understand. It's not you. It's the circumstances."

"We do understand. At least, as much as we can, not being in your shoes." He tapped the keyboard arrow, and another picture slid onto the screen. A photo of an attractive, mature man appeared. "That's Dad."

"My...father?" she whispered, mouth going drier than it had her first day on the radio.

The most ridiculous thing happened then. Tears pushed at the back of her eyelids. She blinked them away.

From beneath a gray cowboy hat, Clint Caldwell smiled into the camera, laugh lines around hazel eyes that matched Wyatt's. Her father had been a big, handsome cowboy. Really handsome. It was easy to see what had attracted her mother, and if Clint was half as nice as his youngest son, Mom would have fallen hard and fast. Like she always did.

"We'd been cutting hay that day," Wyatt said. "It was blazing hot, and Connie drove out to the field with a gallon of iced tea. Emily snapped this with her phone. We didn't know then that it would be one of the last pictures before Dad died."

"He looks so strong and healthy."

"We thought he was." His voice was hushed, sad. "He wasn't perfect, but he was a good man, a great dad who taught us kids right from wrong and to follow Jesus. And of course, how to ride and work cows and run a ranch."

"I wish I'd known him." A good man, even though he'd made a mistake somewhere along the line. A big mistake. Her.

"Your mother never said a word about him? No photos or anything?"

"Nothing." Which meant she was ashamed, of her relationship with Clint, of the daughter they'd had together. "I wonder if he knew about me."

"Absolutely not." Wyatt shook his head, adamant. "He didn't."

"How can you be sure?"

"If Dad had known, you would have been part of his life. Part of our lives."

"Unless my mother refused."

"I suppose that's possible. But Dad wasn't one to give up. He'd have demanded visitation and sent child support."

Or maybe he wanted to keep his dirty little

secret. She didn't say that. No use hurting a family that was trying to reach out to her. Unlike Wyatt, she wasn't convinced that Clint hadn't known about her.

"Mom always had money for anything we needed or wanted, but her career pays well." Had her job been that good? Or had she received a pay-off to keep quiet about the affair?

"Did you grow up in Bayville?" Wyatt asked.

She snapped her gaze to his. Did he know about Aaron? Or was he trying to figure out, as she was, how their father and her mother met? "Ft. Worth area."

Not far from the stockyards, the rodeo arena, the livestock shows. A perfect place for a cowgirl to meet a successful rancher.

AFTER WYATT LEFT, Dallas changed into jeans and sneakers, tossed on her coat, and went for a prayer walk, her way of releasing the anxiety built up by her meeting with Wyatt. An extrovert, she was rarely nervous with people, but this situation had her in knots.

Though the temperature was cold, there was no wind, and the bright sun felt good. As she walked, her prayers wandered from her own situation to

Lawson and his niece, seeking some way to help them. Lawson tried hard with the girl, but Madison needed a woman's example and counsel.

Dallas stopped, aware of the putter of traffic, the racket of a jackhammer somewhere, a distance siren. Was that Lawson's police vehicle? Would he be offended if she offered friendship to the young teen? At least, during the time she was in town getting acquainted with her new family?

She turned around and started back to the hotel, walking faster now, as the idea took root. Was God speaking to her? Or was she looking for any excuse to avoid Bayville and spend more time with the sheriff?

Back inside the hotel room, Dallas called Bethany and filled her in on the last few, crazy days, including the meeting with her half-brother.

Bethany sounded shocked, to say the least. Behind her trendy glasses, Bethany's brown eyes were probably as round as Oreos. "Does your mother know about this?"

"No, and please don't say anything." The thought of Mom's reaction shook her very bones.

"I won't, but discovering who your father is and meeting his family, is pretty significant. You can't keep that a secret."

Bethany was right. Dallas and Mom had always been close. They discussed most everything. Except her father.

Dallas raised a shaky hand to her forehead. "Right now, I need time to unscramble my brain and my emotions. Then, I'll talk to her."

She wasn't looking forward to that moment, but she knew the conversation was necessary. Later.

They spoke a few more minutes, caught up on some other friends, fretted over the job loss and Aaron, and then hung up. Dallas had barely put her phone back on the charger when someone knocked at the door.

She went to the peephole and saw the top of a blond head. "Who is it?"

"Madison."

Madison? What was she doing here?

Dallas opened the door. Without waiting to be invited, Madison schlepped inside and dumped a dirty gray-and-pink backpack on the desk.

"What's going on?" Dallas asked. "Is something wrong? Why aren't you in school?"

The girl gazed around the hotel room, one shoulder lower than the other. "This is a lot nicer than the dumps my dad picks."

"Does your uncle know you're here?"

Madison gave her the *seriously* look. "He's at work. As always. He had some big meeting, so he couldn't pick me up after school."

"You need to let him know where you are."

"I hate school. Did I tell you that?"

"You mentioned it. Did something happen at school today?"

"I hate riding the stinky bus. I'd rather walk. So I walked here."

"Is there a reason you're avoiding my questions?" Dallas asked gently, using her best on-air, coaxing voice.

"Maybe." Madison prowled the small space, looked out the single window, and then collapsed on the bed with a put-upon sigh. "I don't fit in this stupid town."

"What happened?"

There was a long hesitation but Dallas waited her out. Finally, the words gushed forth like a broken fire hydrant.

"There's this girl in my history class." Madison grabbed one of the bed pillows and wadded it against her belly. "So, we're all standing around talking, and she started saying a bunch of stuff about me and my mom."

Oh, the cruelty of teenagers. "Such as?"

"My mom didn't want me. She ran off because I was so stupid and ugly. Stuff like that. Then one of the others said my dad didn't want me either, or he wouldn't have dumped me on my uncle. Even if it's true, it's not their business."

Small town gossip moved fast. "But it hurts anyway, doesn't it?"

Madison got that belligerent expression again, but her eyes slide away. "Just makes me mad. I wanted to smack her in the face."

"I'm glad you didn't."

"Couldn't. Uncle Sheriff would throw me in the dungeon."

"The dungeon?" Dallas said, mildly amused. "Rather draconian of him."

"Yeah. Whatever that means."

Dallas handed her the phone. "Shoot him a text, let him know you're with me."

Madison sat up, blinking. "I can stay?"

"For a while. I did promise to do your eyebrows, didn't I? Then, I'll drive you home. Your uncle promised to cook dinner for us tonight."

"Seriously? For us? Or just for you?"

"Does he really strike you as the kind of man to leave you out?"

Madison swallowed and had the grace to look

sheepish. She stared down at Dallas's cell phone. "I guess not. But it's weird. He's weird."

Dallas narrowed her eyes. If the sheriff was weird, she needed to know about it *now*. "In what way?"

"I mean, why's he nice to me when he didn't want me here in the first place?" Her fingers raced across the keypad and then returned the phone. "I don't get it."

Oh, *that* kind of weird. Good weird.

Dallas pointed toward the desk chair, the only straight back in the room. "Get over here in my beauty spa, and let's talk about it while we tame those eyebrows."

Madison moved at the speed of light. And she almost looked happy doing it.

Maybe the Lord had just opened a door for Dallas to help Lawson's hurting niece.

CHAPTER 7

"*T*hank you for agreeing to come with me."
Dallas put her hand in Lawson's
outstretched one. He was pretty happy about that.

Parked outside the Triple C Ranch, he assisted
the beautiful, delicious-smelling woman from the
cab of his truck. Dallas looked stunning, as always,
in a pretty green dress and those boots that made
him want to look at her legs. Any man would be
proud to be seen with her.

She was an awesome person too. She had to be to
deal so kindly with snarky, moody Madison.

Last night, they'd had an incredible time at his
ranch. Dallas had proved to be a fine horsewoman
and had even given Madison, a complete greenhorn,

a few pointers as they'd ridden slowly to the big pond and back. He'd pointed out the ranch boundaries, his small head of mama cows and the other horses.

She'd seemed impressed, complimenting the place in a way that made him proud of his accomplishments.

Yeah. He definitely hoped this woman stuck around for a while.

When she'd invited him to go with her to meet the rest of the Caldwell clan, he couldn't have refused if he'd wanted to. Thankfully, he hadn't wanted to. "They're fantastic people. You're going to like them."

"At least we have a love of horses in common."

"And probably more than that."

"But I don't look like any of them, you said. I'm the outcast, the odd man out, the secret they didn't know about."

They'd been over this last night.

He took her hand and squeezed. Sure, it was an excuse, but she needed the calming comfort, and he liked touching her soft skin. He knew she was nervous. He was sorry about that, but convinced she'd feel better after she'd discovered how open-hearted her new family could be.

"They're not going to judge you, Dallas. I know them." If they were going to judge anyone, it would have been him after he'd arrested Wyatt's fiancé and tossed her in jail. Lawson winced. On Christmas day, no less. But they hadn't. That was the kind of people they were.

"It all seems...overwhelming." Dallas licked pink lips as they walked up the tall steps to the front door of the Triple C Ranch. "I'm glad they agreed to only dessert and coffee this time, and to save dinner for another night. I'm not ready for that."

"Understandable. This way if you want to escape, we can simply make our excuses and leave. Just give the signal."

She stopped at the door and without ringing the bell, shot him another anxious look. "What's the signal?"

He thought for a second. "If you're not comfortable saying you're ready to leave, how about asking me if Madison had a lot of homework tonight?"

"Okay. Sounds good." She took a deep breath and pushed the bell. Inside, a chime sounded, like a grandfather clock marking time.

He squeezed her hand again and winked. She flashed those blue-green eyes at him, trying to smile. He had the insanely random thought that if they had babies together, the kids would have some amazing blue eyes.

The thought shook him. Dumb. Random. No way that was happening. He liked being a bachelor. Had no time for a family. Just ask the poor kid living on his ranch.

The huge, carved door swung opened, and Wyatt appeared, his usual intensity giving away to a friendly greeting. "Come on in. Glad you could make it. The gang's in the family room."

Dallas flicked another anxious glance at Lawson. He gently touched her back, urging her inside the warm, welcoming home.

Leaning close to her ear, he murmured, "Don't get sick on me again. Defacing private property is a capital offense, and I didn't bring my handcuffs."

His silliness made her smile. She nodded, straightened her spine and followed Wyatt into the house.

DALLAS KNEW Lawson had been kidding, but she seriously thought she might throw up. She'd never been this nervous. What if they hated her on sight? What if someone said something really cruel about her mother? About her? What would she do?

She was so glad Lawson was at her side. His strength and humor were exactly what she needed at the moment. It didn't hurt that under a Wrangler fleece jacket, he looked really handsome in a gray plaid shirt, faded blue jeans and cowboy boots. Nice. Tummy-tingling nice.

They passed through a spotlessly clean living room of dark wood furniture, through an enviable, gleaming kitchen, and toward the voices. Her radio experience picked up the nuances of conversation, the inflections, the innuendoes. So far, so good.

As she entered the room, she saw a sea of faces. Lots of them. Her pulse trembled.

Conversations stopped. Only for a second, but long enough to shoot another jolt of panic through Dallas's bloodstream. Quickly, the noise returned, this time in greetings as two women rose from a leather couch and came toward her. She recognized them from the photos Wyatt had shown her. Connie and Emily.

Connie, a lovely, mature Latina with shots of silver along the sides of mid-length dark brown hair, stretched out her hands. Dallas, not knowing what else to do, took them. They were as warm as the woman's smile.

"Welcome," Connie said, with a Spanish accent. "We have been waiting for you. You are Dallas, no?"

"Yes. Dallas Langley. And you must be Connie." She looked at the other woman. "And you're Emily." My half sister, but she didn't say that part. She'd let the family make the first moves in that respect.

Lawson held her coat while she slid it off. She could feel him hovering nearby, quietly protective. Though it was a by-product of his career, she was touched, and his appeal rating scooted up another notch.

"I showed her some family photos," Wyatt said as he took a seat beside his petite fiancé. Try as she might, Dallas couldn't remember the woman's name. Her little boy either, but he was cute, snuggled in between his mother and Wyatt.

"Forgive me, please, if I falter. This has been a lot to absorb. But," she added quickly, "I'm honored to meet all of you."

From there, she, a woman who made a living talking, didn't know what to say or do other than take a seat next to Lawson on yet another couch, this one in a cushy Apache print. The large room was packed with couples and kids, along with Connie and Gilbert, who were long-time employees but behaved and were treated like family members. That gave her hope that she could at least be friends with her father's other children.

Somehow, she carried on conversations over coffee and dark chocolate cake while being amused by the antics of a set of precocious identical twin girls, Sophia and Olivia, and the well-behaved little boy, Braden, son of Wyatt's fiancé, Marley. She'd picked up the names as she'd listened and watched, but she'd have to work on remembering everyone. If they invited her back. And if she agreed to return.

They were cordial, as Lawson had promised, but she felt an undercurrent of tension. Maybe it was her own insecurities.

Ace, her movie-star gorgeous brother, seemed the most distant, the most watchful. His wife, Marisa kept smoothing a hand over his back as if he needed calming. They made Dallas more nervous than she already was.

She answered their questions and asked a few of her own, though all of them were careful to avoid the main subject—how had she come to exist?

She told them a little about growing up in Texas and her love of horses, knowing this was common ground. She slid in the fact that her mother was a barrel racer of some repute and told them of her own career as a radio announcer. She didn't tell them about her most recent trouble or the lost job. Some things were too personal to share with family she'd only met today.

The tension in the back of her neck was killing her. Was she making a good impression? Did they hate her? And why did she care so much?

Suddenly, she felt Lawson's hand taking hers. She glanced at him. His eyes questioned her. Had she had enough? Did she want to leave?

Sweet man. And he was a cop.

She subtly shook her head and tried to relax, an impossible task, but his touch encouraged her.

Trying to move the conversation away from herself, she said, "Tell me more about our father. I wish I could have known him."

It was the right thing to say.

They filled her in about Clint Caldwell, sharing stories about their father that made him seem almost real. Still, they avoided asking about her mother.

"Once when I was about thirteen and thought I knew everything," Nate said in his gentle way that fit the teddy-bear image Wyatt had painted for her, "Dad bought a stallion to start a new breeding program. He warned all of us to stay away from the new horse until he'd had time to work with it and make sure it was safe."

"But Nate didn't," Emily added. "He thought he was a real wrangler by then."

"Sure, I did," Nate said. "I'd been riding all my life, and we'd owned stallions before."

Dallas leaned forward a little. "What happened?"

One of the twins lifted her arms, and Nate set her on his knee. She kissed his cheek, and the cowboy smooched the top of her dark head. "I learned a valuable lesson."

"And nearly got your daddy killed in the process," Gilbert added, his Native American features wreathed in affectionate annoyance.

"I got the stallion saddled with no problem, led him out into the paddock and climbed aboard." Nate rubbed his chin and grimaced. "The last thing I remember is seeing dad running out of the barn just as I went flying through the air."

"I remember. Real good," Gilbert said. "Connie heard Clint holler and busted out of the house. Clint vaulted the fence into the paddock like an Olympian. By then, the stallion was out of his head, raring, pawing."

"And Nate was under his hooves." Connie looked as if she'd never gotten over the fright.

"I don't remember a thing," Nate said.

"Because you were unconscious, doofus," Ace said, his green eyes poking fun at his brother.

"Unconscious," Gilbert repeated. "Connie was crying and praying in Spanish while Clint stormed that stallion as if he wasn't dangerous. Stallion's hooves got him right across the shoulder."

"Knocked him down, but he got back up. His arm hung to one side." Connie muttered something in Spanish and shook her head. "I knew it was broken."

"That's when you started inside the paddock." Ace pointed to Gilbert.

"Clint yelled at me to stay out. Boss's orders." Gilbert huffed. "Made me plenty mad, so I yelled for the other hands to bring ropes and snuck inside anyway."

"Clint tried to fire you for disobeying orders." Connie's gaze rested on Gilbert, her smile tender. Was there something between the two?

"Yep." A grin split Gilbert's dark face. "But I wouldn't leave. So he unfired me after a few days."

Dallas was intrigued and touched by the devotion running through this family. Her family. "How did you settle the horse and get your—our father—and Nate to safety?"

"Clint kept on talking and walking toward that wild animal. Told me to get the boy out, so I did. Clint had the stallion's reins in his good hand by the time the other men arrived. They roped that crazy stallion, front and back, and worked him into the stall."

"And sold him, not long after," Emily added. "He was beautiful but too high strung for us."

"Dad required surgery, was in a cast and a sling for three months." Nate's lips thinned, expression somber. "I hated that. Felt even worse because he never punished me, never even said a word except, 'Is Nate all right?' But I never disobeyed an order again."

The story touched her. Would Clint have felt the same about her? Would he have protected her with his life? He sounded liked the kind of man who would have, and believing that soothed a lonely place deep inside. She'd never had that bond, that fatherly protection, and she'd missed it. Missed it still.

"He sounds terrific. I wish…" The useless wish stuck in a throat that had grown full and achy, longing for the impossible.

"Dad had his faults," Nate said. "He could be tough and too involved in his work, but we knew he loved us. He proved it that day."

"Were you badly hurt?" Dallas asked.

"Nah. Knocked the breath out of me and gave me a headache. I got my bell rung worse playing football."

"And jumping out of the barn loft." Ace's grin was mischievous.

Nate pointed an index finger at his brother. "That was your fault."

Both men laughed.

The toddler wiggled down from Nate's lap and went in search of her sister, who was playing dollies while Braden drove a Hotwheel around in circles, making motor noises.

The conversation went on around her with Lawson chiming in with a story about her brothers' antics. She enjoyed the tales. They helped her know her siblings better, though it stung a little to have no shared memories.

With the focus and pressure off her, she sipped her coffee. It had cooled, but she didn't complain. She mostly wanted something to do with her hands anyway.

After a couple of hours, conversation lagged, and

she said to Lawson, "We should go. It's getting late. I don't want to outstay my welcome."

"You couldn't," Connie said, "But Lawson says you have been sick, and we talk too much. You should rest now."

"Thank you, Connie. You've been so kind. I realize how awkward this must be for everyone."

"God is good, and He always has a good plan. *Si?*" Connie clasped her hands in front of her like a prayer.

She could easily learn to love this woman. "I believe that too."

"*Bueno.* So, we will be *familia.*" To Lawson, Connie said. "You bring her back soon. When she is ready. Okay? And bring your niece too. I will make *tamal.*"

Lawson grinned that charming grin of his. "For your tamales, anything."

They departed then, the cold night air a jolt after the warm house. Dallas stuck her hands in her coat pockets, glad for Lawson's hand at her elbow as they traversed the steps to the truck.

She'd survived. And she was relieved to find her new family to be friendly, if cautious. She understood that. She was cautious too. But she still didn't know how her parents had met.

. . .

LAWSON GUIDED a shivering Dallas to the dark gray
Silverado, his personal vehicle. He was confident
Dallas's shivering had as much to do with nerves as
the chilly weather, but he started the engine and
cranked up the heater first thing.

When they were on the road, the lights of the
Triple C behind them, he glanced at her. She'd
clasped her hands tightly in her lap.

"Are you all right?"

She nodded, let out a breath. "It was a good meeting, I thought, even if it was uncomfortable."

"You were smooth as butter." But he'd read her
body language, knew she'd been anxious and tense
the entire time. "They liked you."

She angled toward him, the seat belt tugging across
her shoulder. "You think? I couldn't tell. They're nice,
but they have to bear some resentment toward me."

"Why?"

Dallas lifted a palm. "News flash, sheriff. I'm the
illegitimate child of their father, who, according to
you, was a paragon of virtue, devoted to his wife."

Lawson frowned. "You happened after his wife
died. From your age and the date of Cori's death, it's

clear Clint was a widower when he and your mother were involved."

That much was good news. Yet, Clint had also been free to marry and hadn't. Dallas didn't want to let that hurt her, but it did.

"Mom's the only one who can say what really happened, and I'm afraid to tell her that I know."

"Give yourself some time. This is all still very new. Once you get better acquainted with the Caldwells, I think you won't question their intentions, and you'll be proud to talk about them."

"I hope so. At least they didn't try to kill me because I'd inherited a lot of their money or land from our mutual father."

Lawson bit back a snort. "They *are* pretty wealthy, and the Triple C Ranch is one of the biggest spreads in this part of the state."

She groaned. "I was afraid you'd say that."

"But Wyatt is convinced your dad didn't know about you, so there is no inheritance."

"Thank goodness."

This time the snort escaped. "I don't think anyone has ever felt that way about *not* inheriting money before."

"A disputed inheritance is one less thing to worry

about." She rubbed a hand over the back of her neck and squeezed.

"Your head starting to hurt?"

"Neck tension. I get that sometimes when I'm stressed."

"Which seems to be a lot."

"Under the current circumstance and adding a couple of things I've gone through lately, it's explainable, but you're right. I stress too much. God and I are working on it, but I'm not holding up my end of the deal." She stretched her arms out in front of her, shook them out as if to release tension. "Enough about me. Let's discuss your niece."

"Madison?" He shot her a look and then returned his attention to the highway. "Why? What's to discuss?"

"She needs a woman in her life."

He groaned. "I know. And she needs her father too, but neither parent seems inclined."

"Right. Which leads me to an offer."

"Keep talking."

"I'm going to stay in Calypso for a week or two to learn more about my father."

Yes! He almost ran off the road.

"Emily mentioned a nice B and B with better

rates than the hotel, plus breakfast, so I may move there."

What did this have to do with Madison? "The Royal? Nice place. The owner, Countess von Dunenburg, is quirky, but a good sort, and the house is beautiful. On the inside."

"She's a real countess?"

"An American who married a European count years ago when she was a student studying abroad. He died a few years back, so she moved here, bought the house, turned it into a swanky bed and breakfast."

"I'm intrigued."

"Good." And he meant that. He wanted her to like the Royal, like Calypso, fall in love with her family and stick around.

And he must be losing his ever-loving mind.

"So what does any of this have to do with Madison?"

"I want to spend time with her, if you're okay with it."

Okay with it? His heart was leaping out of his chest. "Why would you do that?"

"Because, behind that wall of self-protection is a girl I like, a girl with huge potential, and she responds well to me, most of the time. Maybe I can help while I'm here."

While she was here. Right. *Settle down heart.* Dallas was meant for greener pastures. "To be honest, I'd be grateful."

"I'm not criticizing you, Lawson. I want to be clear about that. Madison likes and respects you, but you remind her of her dad, and she struggles to trust."

"She tell you this?"

"Not outright, but I'm good at reading people, taking what they say and filling in the background. Did you know she's already dealing with a bully at school?"

Lawson clenched the steering wheel. "I'll kick his tail."

Dallas snickered. "The bully is a girl in her class who talks trash and gives Madison a hard time. Madison says she could handle it herself, but she's afraid you'll get mad and send her to foster care."

"She said that?"

"Basically."

"Dumb kid. If she'd just talk to me."

"She's scared of rejection."

"You missed your calling. You know that? You should be a counselor."

Dallas lifted one shoulder, aching a little for what she'd left back in Bayville. "In a way I am. Or I was. And I loved it."

"You should do that again, here in Calypso." He was pathetic. She didn't belong here, wouldn't stay. "I mean, until you find something better. Check out the local station and keep up your skills, gain some new fans."

"I'll think about it."

He'd have to be content with that. For now.

They pulled into the hotel parking lot, and he lifted her out of the truck, more as an excuse to hold her than because she needed assistance.

As he slid her to the pavement, he pulled her a little closer than was necessary and held on, his arms sliding around her waist.

A car passed on the adjacent street, but he and Dallas were protected from prying eyes by his tall truck. The streetlights cast long shadows over the parking area and across Dallas's lovely face. Even in the dark, she glowed with a beauty that took his breath. Inner beauty, outer beauty, Dallas was the complete package.

He was taking no chances tonight. No interruptions, no guests plowing into his romantic moment. No Madison to roll her eyes.

"Before we go inside…" He gazed down into her face. In heels, she was almost as tall as he was. Perfect.

"Yes." Head tilted, Dallas circled his neck with both arms, her lush lips curved and inviting.

He might be a cautious lawman, but he didn't resist the subtle invitation.

His mouth closed over hers, and she sighed as if she'd been waiting for this moment all evening long. He'd been waiting too. Maybe forever.

She was beautiful, passionate, warm and wonderful.

A tender ache rose in Lawson's throat. Strange to feel so much so soon for this woman.

He heard a sound, realized it came from him, a soft, pleased hum. Everything about her called to him.

He tugged her gently closer. As a lawman, he was well disciplined, but Dallas made him feel things. Things that eroded his control. He reined it in, raising his face to gaze into eyes he'd never forget. Not ever.

"Wow," she whispered, bemused, pleased. Her breath tickled his lips. "I wasn't expecting…that."

That explosion of emotion, the exquisite tenderness, the sudden thought that this, *this* was right. And that it mattered. *She* mattered.

"Me either," he whispered, stunned, mesmerized, swamped.

And then Lawson was kissing her again as if only Dallas held the keys to unlock his heart, as if he'd waited for this moment, this woman, all his life.

Man, was he in trouble.

CHAPTER 8

*N*o one answered her knock.

Dallas knocked again and listened for sound inside Lawson's ranch house. Nothing.

She glanced around the empty yard, heard the rustle of the dead grass in the field across the road.

Somewhere a horse whinnied, and a woodpecker jack-hammered a tree.

She hadn't expected Lawson to be home yet, but Madison should be.

A worry niggled at Dallas. Had the moody teen had another run-in with someone at school? Had she forgotten Dallas's promise to drive out after she'd finished moving her things into the Royal Bed and Breakfast?

She pondered for a few moments, listening. The

trees in Lawson's yard were bare and lonely looking, but someone had planted a holly with bright red berries next to the porch. Nearby, a clump of green spears, probably daffodils, pushed out of the cold earth.

The fickle Texas weather was sunny and warmer today, brightening the world, hinting at the spring to come.

Somewhere close, a horse whinnied again.

If she were a teenager with a pasture full of horses, Dallas knew exactly where she'd be.

Stepping off the porch, she walked around to the end of the long house and peered toward the outbuildings in back. Though Madison was not in sight, Dallas headed out there anyway. As she opened the gate leading into the paddock, she heard Madison's voice, soft and low.

Dallas eased through the gate, closing it quietly behind her, and paused at the edge of the barn. A metal shed with an open front protruded from the back of the main barn, a loafing shed. Madison was there, brushing the mane of Lawson's aging mare, Sadie. As she brushed, she talked, her voice gentle.

"He hasn't even called to ask about me," she was saying. "If I had a kid, I'd at least do that."

Oh, that poor girl. Dallas's heart twisted like a

pretzel. She remained as still as possible, listening to the teen pour her troubles on the sweet old horse.

"Uncle Sheriff's okay, I guess. He makes sure I have food and whatever. And he never has forgot about me. Not even once. Dad does all the time."

As if she were having a conversation with a human, Madison paused to look into the mare's liquid brown eyes. The horse calmly gazed back.

"Uncle Sheriff even gave me some money in case I need it. I mean, for what? Weird, huh? Giving out random money. Who does that?"

Madison brushed a long stroke down the mare's shoulder, bending toward her hooves. The mare turned a graceful head and nuzzled the girl's back.

Madison straightened, one palm resting on the animal's side. "I wish Dad was like him."

There was such a plaintive tone in the girl's voice that Dallas ached for her. But if Madison knew she'd heard, she'd feel betrayed, and Dallas could lose their fragile connection. Madison didn't need to lose anyone else.

Silently Dallas exited the barnyard. Then, to warn of her arrival, she clattered the metal gate as loudly as she could and called, "Madison, are you out here?"

"In the loafing shed," came the reply.

Dallas joined her. "Nice of you to brush Sadie."

"She's a sweet girl. I think she likes me."

"She does. See how she leans toward you with her head down, and her lower lip is loose and relaxed?"

"Yeah?"

"That means she's comfortable with you. She trusts you."

Madison considered that for a second. "Uncle Sheriff says she's going blind."

Dallas slid a hand along the mare's neck and up to her ears for a gentle scratch. She'd missed this contact with the equine world. "Sad."

"He puts medicine in her eyes, but the vet says it's not working. Eventually, she'll be in the dark." Madison turned a worried gaze toward Dallas. "What if she can't find the barn or her feed or water? What will happen to her?"

"Have you asked Lawson?"

"No. But Jenny, this girl in my class, said her dad sells the ones that get too old to be useful." Her gray eyes were troubled. "And then they're like, slaughtered and turned into dog food or something gross like that."

"Do you actually think your uncle would do that?"

Madison shrugged. "I don't know. He's a cop."

Dallas chuckled. Hadn't she stereotyped him the same way? "Who happens to care about his animals." *And you, too, if you'd only realize it.*

"I'd take care of Sadie forever if he'd let me." The girl kicked at a dried cow chip. "I mean, if I'm still around."

"Would you like that? To stay in Calypso with your uncle and take care of Sadie?"

Madison stared down at her feet. "My dad's supposed to come get me soon."

Then where was he? The irresponsible creep. "That's not what I asked."

"Doesn't matter, does it? Kids don't exactly get a say." The angry tone was back. "And why should you care anyway? You won't be around either."

The accusation struck Dallas in the chest.

Madison spun and threw the brush at the barn. It bounced off, landing in the dirt. The mare skittered.

The girl softened, instantly contrite. With a kiss to the side of Sadie's muzzle, she murmured, "Sorry, Sadie. I didn't mean to scare you. I'm just stupid."

"Madison." Dallas touched the girl's arm. "There's nothing stupid about you. You may be confused about some things, and understandably so, but you're smart, pretty, and most of all, caring. Not a bit stupid." She winked. "Just ask Sadie."

"I guess," Madison said without much conviction. "But if I'm all that, why don't my parents like me?"

"The problem isn't with you. It's with them." Even to her, the words sounded like platitudes.

"Right. Like I believe that."

Dallas lifted her face to the sun, pondering what to say. Her personal situation was still raw and unsettled, but if it would help Madison…

"Did I tell you that I grew up without a father?" she asked softly. "Never met him, didn't know his name. All my life, I wondered why he didn't love me, why he'd gone away and left me and my mother."

"I didn't know that." Madison looked at her with interest.

"That's why I'm here in Calypso. I found my dad, but it's too late to know him. He died."

"That stinks."

"It does. But you know what? Not having a dad in my life may have affected me in some ways, but I had a great mom. She taught me to dream and to make goals and pursue them."

"Is that how you got into radio?"

"It is. With Mom's encouragement. She noticed my interest and talent before I did."

"Yeah, well, I don't have a mom *or* a dad."

"But you have your uncle, and Lawson cares deeply about you and won't let you down."

"You don't know that for sure. You're just into him, so you think he's all perfect and everything."

Into him. What a clueless teenage way of putting the most glorious emotion into words.

The thought caught Dallas off guard. Where had that come from? She couldn't, wouldn't fall in love with a small-town sheriff. Like him, yes. Enjoy his company, absolutely. Love him, no way. She still had those goals she'd made and a career ladder to climb. Love would have to wait.

"I think you're wrong. Lawson cares about you, or you wouldn't be here."

"Maybe. I don't know. He's all right, I guess."

Madison quietly picked up the thrown brush and put it away. Dallas could tell she was considering their conversation and thinking about her uncle.

She led the mare through the gate into the open pasture. Lawson's gelding, Tripp, ambled toward them, head up, and whinnied.

Sadie perked up, her ears forward.

"Go on, girl," Madison turned loose of the mare's halter and gave her neck a pat. "Your buddy's here. I'll bring apples after dinner."

When the gelding whinnied again, Sadie bolted toward him, kicking out her hind legs like a young horse.

Madison laughed and leaned both forearms on top of the gate to watch the pair play. The wind tickled the ends of her long blond hair.

Suddenly Dallas saw more parallels between herself and Madison than blond hair and their lack of a parent. Her horse had been her best friend. Some days, when she hadn't been confined to her room by macho cop, she'd ride for hours, pouring out her anger at her stepdad to the only creature that would listen without judgment. The way Madison had done today.

Tugging her jacket closed, Dallas joined the young girl in watching the animals romp. They stood silently, side by side, two blondes with a father wound and a love of horses.

LAWSON SAW them as he drove into the yard and parked the department's SUV. The two females in his life, fair hair stirring in the light breeze as they peered out into the pasture.

He got a funny hitch beneath his ribcage, one of those feelings that somehow this was meant to be—

Dallas and Madison, here on his ranch. As if their presence made his life complete.

Strange thoughts, out-of-character feelings. But good, too.

Was he mellowing in his not-so-old age?

He hopped out of the vehicle and followed his heart to the barnyard.

"Hey, girls."

Both swung around to greet him. Both smiled.

He strode to the fence and squeezed between them, tossing an arm over each one. Madison stiffened for a moment, but then she relaxed, leaning into him. Dallas smiled up at him as if he'd done something to please her.

So he did. He kissed her. Quick and light, a sweet hello.

"If you kiss *me*," Madison growled. "I'll throat punch you."

But when Lawson glanced down at her, she was grinning.

He gave her neck an affectionate squeeze.

"How was your day?" Dallas asked.

"Routine. How was yours? Did you get moved to the B & B?"

"I did."

For some reason, this simple act of moving her

belongings from a hotel to the bed and breakfast thrilled him. He didn't know why. A B & B was just as temporary as a hotel. "Sorry I couldn't get loose to help out. I gotta hire an undersheriff soon."

"I didn't have that much to move, Lawson. It was no big deal."

It was to him. "What did you think of the Countess?"

Dallas chuckled. "She's lovely and fun."

"What was she wearing?" His mouth lifted in a knowing grin.

Madison slid from beneath his arm and stared at him aghast. "That's a weird question. Even for you."

Lawson tugged on a lock of her hair. It was clean and silky against his fingers, a big change from when she'd arrived. "That's because you haven't met the Countess. But you will now that Dallas is staying at the Royal."

"Can I?"

"May I." Dallas corrected. "And yes, you may. Anytime your uncle says it's all right."

"Tomorrow?" Madison's face was alight with eagerness. Dallas was her most admired person at the moment. Lawson certainly understood that. "I can walk down there from school. You won't have to pick me up or send one of the officers or anything."

He tried to be available whenever school dismissed, but sometimes a police call kept him away and someone else had to see her safely home. A few times he'd imposed upon Dallas, and twice Madison had had to ride the bus, which she hated and let him know in no uncertain terms. He'd told her to deal with it, but he understood. School buses weren't the best place for a new kid with a chip on her shoulder. Once he got her attitude under control, she might actually enjoy the ride.

"If you're busy," Dallas said, turning toward him in a move that forced him to drop his arm from her shoulders. He wasn't thrilled about that. "I can pick her up."

"Thanks. I'll text you tomorrow."

"Awesome," Madison said. "Oh, and can I go to Jenny's house on Saturday? She invited me, and we can hang out and ride her horses and stuff if the weather's good. Her mom said it was okay."

Madison had made a friend? Now, that was progress! In fact, this evening, she behaved more like a normal teen than he'd ever seen. Was she settling in? Or was it Dallas's influence?

"Who are her parents?"

His niece rolled her eyes. Just once, Lawson

wished they'd get stuck that way. But only long enough for her to stop doing it.

"How would I know? You're the law. Don't you know everybody?"

"Does Jenny have a last name?"

"Patterson. Her dad works at the post office or something."

"Don Patterson. I know him, see him practically every day. Let me talk to him tomorrow and make sure it's okay."

"Jenny said it was." Madison's hackles rose. "Don't you believe me?"

"Hey." Dallas put a hand on Madison's stiff shoulder. "Of course, he believes you. But talking to the parents is the polite and proper way of getting invited to someone's house. Plus, he's keeping you safe. It's one of those things that make adults feel better."

His niece's expression slowly changed to compliance. "Oh. Okay. That's cool, I guess. But can I tell Jenny that you said yes if her dad says yes?"

"Sure."

"Can I borrow your cell? I want to call her."

Lawson fished his phone from a pocket and handed it over.

"If I had my own phone," she said, "I wouldn't have to bother you."

"I'll think about it." Was thirteen old enough to own an expensive phone?

Madison gave him a long, questioning look, then took his cell and walked toward the house.

"The keys to a young girl's heart," Dallas said softly.

"What's that? A cell phone?"

"Letting her grow while also keeping a rein on her. She's never had that."

"She fights it."

"But she also wants it. Your involvement says you care."

"She's never had that either. Not fully. Bryce probably loves her, but he loves himself the most. As far as I can tell, his daughter has only been an afterthought in his life."

"I'm glad she has you." Dallas slipped her hand in his. "She is too, even if she can't say it yet."

"I hope you're right. I'm kind of getting attached to the little space alien."

She smiled. "Me, too."

"Kind of getting attached to someone else too." He lifted her fingers and kissed them, hopeful of a like-minded reply.

"I know what you mean." Dallas's voice was low and pensive as she stared off toward the house and the girl now entering the back door, the cell phone against her ear.

Pondering the noncommittal comment, Lawson decided now was not the time to push. He steered to safer ground. "I ran into Wyatt and Nate in town. They mentioned you."

"What did they say?"

"Their first impressions were really good. They whole family wants to get to know you better. You're invited to dinner tomorrow night and to church on Sunday with dinner after."

"Emily said the same this morning on the phone. She seems super nice."

"She is. So…are we going?"

She bumped his side. "We? Is there a frog in your pocket?"

"Old joke. And yes, *we*. I'm invited too. Are you complaining?"

"Not at all." She looped her arms over his shoulders. "Having a police escort keeps me from getting a ticket."

"I still owe you one." Expression teasing, he looped his arms loosely around her waist.

"Police brutality."

He laughed and kissed her nose.

"Uh-uh." she said, and lifted her lush, pink mouth to his.

Who was he to refuse? All day, he'd thought about her, about the way kissing her rocked his universe. Every single time.

So, he let her rock it again. And, if her bemused, well-kissed expression was an indicator, he did a little world-rocking himself.

After another kiss or three, they stood together in the barn lot, sun bright and horses grazing peacefully. It was a pleasant scene, a good feeling, and Lawson felt a contentment he hadn't known was missing.

A few moments of quiet passed before Dallas said, "May I ask you something?"

"Anything."

"Emily mentioned something called "The Sanctuary" where her parents are buried. Do you know the place?"

"I do. The Caldwell boys were my best friends growing up, especially Nate. I worked summers for the ranch, too. We rode all over the Triple C, including the Sanctuary. It's kind of a sacred place to them."

Dallas nodded. "Emily said her parents are buried there. She asked if I'd like to visit our father's grave."

"Would you?"

"I think so, but..." Two small furrows wrinkled the space between her eyebrows.

"But what?"

"Visiting a grave is such a personal thing. I'd rather go without them the first time, but I can't tell them that. It would hurt their feelings."

"They'll understand. In fact, it might be easier for them, as well."

"Will you go with me?"

He'd go to the moon and back for her. "If that's what you want."

"It is."

Lawson loved that she wanted his company, and only his company, in such a hallowed place. "Does Saturday work for you? The weather is supposed to be decent, and I'm off duty."

She nodded, her pale hair snatching diamonds from the sun. "We could go while Madison visits Jenny."

"Sounds like a good plan."

She looped her arm through his, face upturned so that Lawson's breath was caught short in his throat.

"Thank you. There are a lot of things like this I

need to do before I go back to Texas. You make everything so much easier."

The sun went behind a cloud, the pleasure of the day darkened.

Go back to the Ft. Worth area. Lawson knew that was the plan. A woman like Dallas didn't stick around small towns, even if she liked the sheriff. And she did. He knew she did. But not as much as he liked her.

Sooner or later, Dallas would leave, and he was very afraid she'd take his heart with her.

CHAPTER 9

*D*allas was silent as she walked beside Lawson through a field and into the woods of The Triple C Sanctuary, a large expanse of wilderness the Caldwells had set aside as a personal game refuge.

Lawson, because of his close friendship with the Caldwell family, had received permission to bring her here, though not surprisingly he owned a key to the huge white gate marked *Triple C Ranch*. The posted signs along the fence were clear. *Private. Keep out.* Family only. Which, apparently, now included her.

She was still trying to decide how she felt about that.

"It's mostly wild land and woods, some creeks

and canyons." His voice was hushed to match her mood. "As boys, we explored most of it."

This time of year, the land looked dead and empty, but in a month or two, when dogwoods and redbuds bloomed, it would be lovely.

"Where is my father buried?"

"Through here." Lawson pointed toward a stand of evergreens. "There's a clearing. You'll see."

As if he felt her tension, Lawson took her hand, smoothing a thumb over its back again and again. He was intuitive like that, a trait she admired.

She admired many things about this man. He was thoughtful and kind and unselfish, and about as masculine a man as she'd ever met. Strong and protective. A real keeper.

For someone.

In moments, they stepped through the trees. Dallas sucked in a gasp.

Lawson turned his head to look at her. "Beautiful, isn't it?"

"And unexpected." Before them was a clearing containing a small church, lovely and well-maintained. Its arching roof seemed to point straight up to heaven.

"Clint built this. Your dad."

The term still caused a drop in her stomach. Dad. Her dad. Clint Caldwell. "Why?"

Lawson shifted, looking uncomfortable. "Cori was dying of cancer. He built it for her."

Cori, her father's wife. A mix of emotions swirled inside Dallas. To build a chapel like this in such a beautiful setting, her father must have been devoted to his wife. Which brought her back to the question: How had she, Dallas Langley, come to exist?

"Did she live long enough to see it?"

"She did and came here often, according to what I've been told. I was too young to remember. But Gilbert says she prayed here nearly every day and maybe found some much needed peace during her illness."

"Undoubtedly, she felt her husband's love in this place."

Dallas wanted to resent the fact that her father had loved his wife so deeply and loved her mother only long enough, only strong enough, to father a child, but she couldn't. A man who could love that much was worth knowing. Respect, however, was another matter.

Had he known about his other daughter? That was the question that haunted her.

"Want to go inside?" Lawson asked, leading the way toward the chapel.

"Yes."

With the quiet hush of woods and birdsong around them, they stepped through the unlocked door into a tiny space. Four pews with an altar in front of them, and against the front wall, a plain wooden cross.

"Skylights," she mused, staring up at the ceiling where the day's pale sunlight seeped through glass.

"No electricity. Just skylights and windows."

"It's beautiful. Simple but lovely, and I feel a... reverence. Don't you?"

"Every time I step inside, it's like God is here, waiting. When I was a teenager hanging with the Caldwell boys, I used to sneak off from the others and come here just to sit and feel that holy presence. Occasionally, when something particularly ugly has happened in my job, I still come here. That's why they gave me a key."

Lawson's words moved her. In her experience, not many men, particularly tough cops, would admit such a need for God.

"Are the graves nearby?" Her heart pinched a little to think of meeting her father for the first time at his graveside.

"Out back. Come on, I'll show you."

They exited the chapel, their feet making soft, swishing sounds against the sleeping grass. Except for a single cawing crow, a hush settled over the meadow.

At the edge of the building, Lawson paused and turned her toward him. "Are you ready for this?"

She nodded.

"Would you rather be alone? I can wait inside the chapel."

Thoughtful, sweet man. "No. Come with me. Please."

He held out his hand. She took it, and together they made the turn around the building. Immediately, she saw the graves. One large black granite stone with a pair of entwined white doves on top marked them both.

Dallas walked closer, grateful for Lawson's quietly supportive presence. He let go of her hand, and when she glanced at him in question, he dipped his chin. "Go ahead. Say hello to your dad. I'm right here."

Her dad. A thick lump formed in her throat. For several seconds, she couldn't speak, so she nodded and walked around the stone to the names. Her focus fell on only one.

"Clint Nathaniel Caldwell," Dallas managed to murmur, almost to herself, but to him too. Her father. "Hello."

She touched the letters, letting one finger slide over the rough granite.

Did you know about me?

The unanswerable question stuck in her throat.

Someone had recently placed purple and white flowers in the headstone vases. And the area around the graves appeared neat and well cared for.

Her father's kids had loved him, loved him still and respected him in death. Would she have loved him, too? Would he have loved her?

Secrets. They never brought any good. And now, the secret Clint Caldwell had kept from his family stood at his gravesite. Wishing she'd known him, wishing she could have loved him in person, this mysterious man she'd longed for her entire life.

LAWSON WATCHED the conflicting emotions come and go on Dallas's face. This couldn't be easy, but she needed to do this.

He stood with his hands folded, taking his cues from her. It was important to give her space, but it was important, too, to be here if she needed him.

When she glanced up, eyes swimming, he took that as a need and crossed the short expanse of grass to reach her.

"He would have loved you so much."

A watery smile met his comment. "Do you always know the right things to say?"

If he did, he'd spill his guts and ask her to stay indefinitely in Calypso.

"Clint would have been proud of all you've accomplished, of how beautiful and kind you are."

"Thank you. It helps to believe he wouldn't have been ashamed of me."

"I knew him, Dallas. Clint wasn't like that."

She sniffed, nodded, putting on her brave front as she pressed fingertips against her eyelids "I didn't expect to feel this emotional."

Lawson let Dallas set the pace. She needed time for her feelings and thoughts to evolve and settle. So he waited.

The moments lengthened as birds rustled in the trees along the edge of the clearing. When at last she turned away from the headstone, Lawson drew her toward him.

She rested her head against his shoulder and said on a sigh, "Thank you."

Lawson kissed the top of her head, inhaled her

sweet fragrance, and then, without conversation, led the way back to the truck.

As he helped her up into the cab, she gave him a soft smile that squeezed his heart. No words, only that smile. And it was enough.

Driving the Silverado deeper into the sanctuary to a particularly pretty bend in Willow Creek, Lawson paused beside a weeping willow. When Dallas gazed at him in question, he said, "Let's walk. I think you'll enjoy it." She needed it too.

Dallas nodded. Again, no words, but he could see her beginning to settle as he continued along the trail. The tiny furrow eased from her forehead, and her hands unclenched in her lap. Once, she looked up and out the window to watch a red-tailed hawk circle overhead.

Her lovely profile drew his attention. He had to discipline his mind to remain focused on the bumpy, grassy trail.

Lawson realized then that he could sit in silence or in conversation with Dallas Langley and be perfectly content. Simply being with her was enough to fill him from the inside out.

Saying goodbye was going to hurt.

When he'd parked near the creek, they got out,

and Lawson took the picnic basket Connie had packed for him from the back of the truck.

"Connie insisted," he said when Dallas appeared surprised. "In case we get stranded in the backwoods for days and days."

The silly comment seemed to lighten her pensive mood. Mouth forming in an O, she pressed a hand against each cheek. "I can't get stranded. I didn't bring my makeup bag."

They both chuckled. He loved her humor.

"I've seen you with and without makeup."

"Don't remind me."

"You're beautiful either way."

"Oh." Her face wreathed in pleasure, she tugged her jacket closed.

"Too cold?"

"No. I'm fine. This is…nice. I've never had a winter picnic."

She'd have her first with him. He liked that idea.

They walked, talking a little but mostly noticing the natural world around them. The air was chilly today, but not bitter, and the Texas wind kinder than usual. It was a fair day, as late winter days go.

Lawson ducked beneath some low hanging branches and stopped next to the creek. Dallas followed.

"This is one of my favorite spots in the Sanctuary," he said. "Willow Creek."

Water bubbled in the wide stream, clear and lazy, the way he felt sometimes when he'd come here. The peaceful sound relaxed him. The overhanging trees sheltered him. He could hide out here with his thoughts and prayers, talk out loud to God and never be seen or heard by another human. He was grateful for that, and as a busy sheriff who saw the harder side of life, he sometimes needed the solitude. The beauty helped wash away the ugliness.

"I can see why."

After taking a blanket from the basket, Lawson spread it on the ground and set the basket there.

"When I come here alone, I feel as if I'm the only person on earth. Just me and God."

"You must get a lot of thinking done here."

"This is where I sort out all the problems of the world." He smirked. "Of Calypso County, anyway."

He didn't add that he'd come here yesterday to make sure the area was safe and clean. And to pray and ponder what he was going to do about his growing feelings for Dallas Langley.

DALLAS STROLLED CLOSER to the creek, feeling the

peace and quiet ebb and flow with the water. As she gazed across at the tangle of brambles and low hanging willows that gave the creek its name, she understood why Lawson liked to come here. A person could let go of a lot of stress in a location like this.

A cottontail hopped out and then stood frozen, its shiny eyes staring at her. She slowly turned her head toward Lawson and pointed.

He came up beside her, his shoulder brushing hers. He said nothing. He was good that way. Silent in the right moments. Warm and funny at other times.

The bunny rabbit turned and casually hopped back into the brambles.

"Oh, no. I scared him off."

"Nah, he simply had better things to do."

So did Lawson, but he was here with her. He'd taken his Saturday off and given it to her, to make things easier for her,

Dallas plucked a dry leaf from the ground at her feet and twirled it in her fingers. "I never really liked cops."

Lawson dipped away from her, a hand over his heart, his eyes wide in fake dismay. "I'm crushed. I thought everyone loved cops."

"Seriously. I couldn't stand anyone even remotely connected with law enforcement."

"Now, you're scaring me." His mouth lifted so she knew he teased. "Exactly how long is your rap sheet?"

"Short. Very short. As in nonexistent."

"Except for defacing Calypso's public sidewalks." He pointed at her. "And speeding."

"There is that." She studied the leaf in her hands. It was crisp and brown, completely dead, but still lovely in its own way. "It's just that I've been let down a few times by police officers, particularly my stepdads."

"They were cops? Both of them?"

"Unfortunately. My mom had a thing for men in uniform." And cowboy boots, apparently. "One guy didn't last long, but the other stuck around for several years. He was a jerk. To me, anyway. Mom refused to see it, for a long time." Dallas rolled her eyes. "She was always that way when she was in love."

Blinded by attraction. Was that what had happened with Mom and Clint Caldwell?

Lawson stiffened. "This guy didn't abuse you, did he?"

The man looked absolutely lethal—in her defense—and Dallas quivered a little with the thrill of it.

"Not in the way you mean. But I spent more time in home jail than I care to admit. My stepdad was a swaggering, overly macho cop who ruled with an iron fist and had the scary muscles to back it up. Granted, my obnoxious teenage perspective was likely skewed, but I despised the guy." She released the leaf to the earth to join its companions. "After too many years, Mom finally realized he was a loser and kicked him out, but by then, I had a very bad opinion of the law."

"I'm sorry." He stepped closer, leaves crunching beneath his boots, and she thought for a minute he might kiss her. She was disappointed when he didn't. "All cops are not like that. Most are good guys, keeping the peace, without much swagger. The job will suck it out of you."

"That bad?"

"Sometimes, but it's the best job in the world when I can help someone."

"Like Madison."

"Madison is a different tale. She's kin. But Lord knows, I'm trying."

Dallas thought now was a good time to tell him about the girl's connection with the horse. "She's all bottled up inside, Lawson. I remember being like that as a teenager fighting with my stepdad. Having my horse to talk to, to groom, to ride off into the quiet woods, made a difference."

"I understand that."

She turned toward him then and put a hand on each of his muscular arms. "I thought you would. She's worried about Sadie going blind."

"So am I." Lawson smoothed her hair away from her face, his touch sending little twinkles of pleasure over her skin.

Dallas leaned in, letting her cheek rest against his tough, manly palm. "What will you do with her?"

"Madison? Or Sadie?" He slid his hands down and over her shoulders before letting them fall to his sides.

Too bad. She loved his touch, loved being this close to him. Loved the mellow, easy feeling his company always brought.

"Both," she answered, "but I meant the horse. Madison's worried she'll go to slaughter."

"Sadie's been with me a long time. She's earned her keep." He turned toward the picnic basket. "She'll live out her life on my ranch."

Dallas followed along, settling across from him on the soft gray blanket. He'd have a hard time getting the leaves and sticks off this one. "I hope you tell that to Madison."

"I will." He flipped up the lid on the basket.

"I overheard her fretting about her dad." She accepted a thermos he offered.

"She misses him," Lawson said.

"Maybe." Unscrewing the thermos cap, Dallas breathed in the aroma of coffee. "But I think she's more worried that he'll take her away."

Lawson's hand paused on the edge of the basket. "She tell you that?"

"Not directly. I'm good at reading between the lines, remember?" She poured coffee into two foam cups. "How would you feel about that?"

"You're sounding like a shrink again." Lawson finished emptying the basket. "But to answer your question, I've given the problem of her delinquent dad and her a lot of thought, and I'm not sure. I'm a bachelor, and my job is demanding of my time, but if she went with Bryce, I'd worry."

"And maybe miss her too?"

"Probably. Even if she is snarky and rude most of the time."

She handed him one of the cups. "Learned behaviors can be unlearned."

"Says Dr. Dallas." He gave her a crooked grin.

"For what it's worth, I agree with you. She's better than she was in the beginning."

"I think so too. We had a good talk the other day, and when she got upset, she apologized. Not to me, but to Sadie."

"It's a start." He pulled out a bag of chips. "Okay, enough about me and my niece. Let's talk about you. Have you discussed your dad with your mother yet?"

She fidgeted with the cup, circling a finger around the rim. Steam moistened her fingertip. "Not yet. I did tell her about my brief hospitalization and that I'm staying in Calypso for a while."

"Did the town name ring a bell to her?"

"If it did, she didn't react." Dallas set the cup on a flat spot in the grass. "I also hinted that I might look around for a job while I'm here."

"Seriously?" Was that hope flaring in his blue, blue eyes?

"I stopped by the local station this morning. They run a nice ship. Small, but professional and progressive."

"Why would you even consider a little station?"

Dallas gave him a sharp look. Didn't he want her around? "A girl's got to have a job somewhere, and after what happened in Bayville..."

She let the thought trail away, hoping he hadn't picked up on it.

"After *what* happened?"

She should have known. Lawson was a cop. Cops don't miss clues as big as the one she'd just dropped.

Was she ready to tell him about Aaron?

"You being a cop, I figured you'd know. Thought you would have checked me out by now."

He shook his head. "That would be a real romance killer."

"So, you haven't? My stepdads ran background checks on everyone."

"I'm not them."

No, he wasn't. He was a conundrum, a wonderful, anomaly in her understanding of cops.

"So," he said. "Are you going to tell me? Or is it none of my business."

After a nano second's hesitation, Dallas decided it was time. She wanted him to know. If Lawson judged her the way some had, she'd know once and for all that he wasn't the man she thought he was.

"I was dating a guy. Things were fine for a few months, but he starting getting possessive. Overly so. To the point he wanted to know where I was and what I was doing every day."

"Abusive?" He said the word mildly, but the look

in his eyes was protective, lethal even. The message was clear. Beneath the cowboy's humor and friendliness was a man who'd defend her with his life.

A tremor ran through Dallas. She was a strong, independent woman, but with Lawson she felt a security she hadn't known was missing.

"If you mean, did Aaron hit me, no. He was just needy, I think." She looked up in the trees and shook her hair back, clearing her head of the images that always came when she thought about Aaron. "Maybe I should have been more understanding. I don't know, but I started feeling smothered and broke things off."

"He didn't take it well." Watching her over the rim, Lawson sipped at his coffee cup.

"Not at all." She sucked in a breath, blew it out, realized she'd started to tremble inside. "Maybe I don't want to talk about this after all."

Instead of trying to convince her, Lawson set aside his coffee and repositioned himself next to her. Putting an arm around her shoulders, he hugged her close to his side. "Okay. Your call. But know I'm here if you need me."

He understood. He got it. And this was Lawson. No way would he accuse her or suspect anything except exactly what she told him to be true. Lawson would never look at her with eyes of disgust or anger or suspicion. She could trust him.

The truth of that pushed away her last bit of anxiety.

Drawing strength from Lawson's strong, solid presence, Dallas continued. "Aaron started harassing me. He called or texted constantly, so much that I considered changing my number. He begged me for another chance, promising to do better. Fifty or more times a day."

"Which only made you more certain you'd done the right thing by ending it."

"Exactly." She raised a shaky hand to her head. A tiny pulse beat had started deep inside her brain. "Then, he started calling my radio show, sometimes more than once a night. The first few times, I talked to him as I would any other caller. Then, as he became pushier, I stopped accepting his call-ins. When I'd see his name on the screen, I'd reject it and go to the next caller. After that, he began driving by my house at all hours."

"I've been in law enforcement long enough to know you were in trouble. Did you call the police?"

A bitter taste came to her mouth. Another reason she disliked cops. "Oh, yes. I called. They suggested a restraining order, so I got one."

"And things got worse?"

"At first, no. Aaron seemed to get the message. I didn't hear from him for over a week and was starting to breathe easier."

"You let your guard down."

"Yes, and that's when it happened. The worst thing, more terrible than I could ever have imagined."

"You're shaking." Lawson turned her into his chest. "You don't have to talk about this. I can find out for myself."

Too many people had misconstrued the facts, including the media and social networks. No way was she letting him learn the story from skewed reports.

Against his cotton-scented shirt, she murmured, "I want you to hear it from me."

She pressed a hand on either side of his solid, dependable chest and backed away. Saying the words was hard. She needed some space.

"About a month ago, I was at work, doing my show. We had a good show that night with lots of interesting callers. I was having a great time and let down my guard."

"The guy called in again."

"Yes. Except he didn't call from his normal

number, so I didn't recognize it, and he used his middle name."

"So you let him on the air."

She nodded, trembling now as she had that night. "All he said was, 'You're making me do this.' And then….he shot himself."

CHAPTER 10

*L*awson's heart jolted so hard, he lost his breath. The words echoed around him, obscene, defiling the pristine wilderness.

Not that. Anything but that.

Lawson remained still, controlling his emotions, letting Dallas's tears dampened his shirt. She'd been through too much. This wonderful woman. As instinctively as he knew how to ride a horse, Lawson knew that Dallas would suffer blame and self-doubt.

"It wasn't your fault."

He felt her nod against his chest. "That's what I keep telling myself, but, Lawson, what if I hadn't taken the call? What if I'd done something differently? Could I have saved his life? He wasn't a horrible person. I never wished him dead."

"Of course you didn't. You wouldn't. You're not like that. But he made the choice, not you."

"I know. I know." She straightened, sitting back. Tears glimmered in her beautiful, anguished eyes. "But did my behavior, my rejection, drive him to suicide?"

"No," he said emphatically. "Get that out of your head. You bear no blame. None."

She sniffed, sighed. "I wish the media agreed with you."

Lawson touched the tears on her cheeks. "Things get twisted sometimes, especially on social media mania."

"Someone even uploaded the call to Facebook. It was quickly taken down, of course, but not before too many people heard it and started wondering what I had done."

"And you let their comments and suspicions get to you."

"How could I not? It was big news *everywhere* in Bayville. So big it leaked into the Dallas press." Her bottom lip trembled, tearing at him.

What she'd been through was too hard, too terrible. "I'm sorry. So sorry you went through that." Again he said, "But it was not your fault."

Reaching into the picnic basket, he took out a

napkin and blotted her cheeks. She took it from him and finished the job.

"So," she said, "that's why I lost my job."

"They fired you because some unbalanced man was stalking you?" he asked, incredulous.

"Bad for business, my boss said. Advertisers ran scared, and a radio station can't function without its advertisers."

"That's lousy." Made him mad all over. His blood boiled at the injustice.

"I thought so too." She offered a brave, if watery smile. "But here I am."

He wasn't sorry about that part. If not for being fired, he'd never have met her.

Lawson realized then, as he sat next to her on a blanket in the wilderness with the creek trickling peacefully past, that he'd done the unthinkable. He'd fallen in love. With a woman on her way to somewhere else.

THE NEXT TUESDAY EVENING, Lawson heard laughter as soon as he arrived home from work. His two girls were here. Where he wanted them both to stay. He still couldn't fathom how he'd come to care so much for both of them in such a short time, but he had.

Maybe because he saw Madison through Dallas's eyes, and he saw Dallas through the eyes of a man in love.

Love. Something he'd never considered as important or necessary. But today, it was as necessary as his next breath.

Without stopping at the house to change out of his uniform, he headed to the corrals. The two females were with the horses almost every evening if the weather was nice like today.

Madison was on Sadie, circling the pen, while Dallas, in blue jeans and a pink hoodie, her hair in a ponytail that made her look as young as his niece, offered instruction and advice. She was an excellent rider and making a good rider out of Madison. His niece was finally comfortable on horseback. By spring, the three of them could trail ride together.

The thought caught him up short. By spring, Dallas would be gone. Maybe Madison would be too. He'd be alone again, something he'd never minded before. Something he'd actually preferred.

Alone didn't sound so good today.

Dallas waved from the spot where she leaned against the metal fence.

Eagerly, Lawson joined her. "She's looking good out there."

"She is, isn't she?" Pleasure brightened Dallas's cheeks. "I'm proud of her. She's come a long way."

"Both in riding and attitude."

"Is she better with you, too?"

"Yep. Last night, she'd done the dishes and had started the laundry by the time I got home. You wouldn't have anything to do with her sudden helpfulness, would you?" He stared down into her face, happy for the excuse to look at her.

"I might have hinted."

"You're a good influence."

"So are you."

"Even though I'm a cop?" he teased, remembering what she'd told him at the Sanctuary.

He also remembered her heartache, and had prayed for her to believe that she'd done nothing to cause Aaron's suicide. After the telling, she'd seemed to feel better as if she was relieved to talk to someone about it. He was glad he'd been the one.

Dallas smiled, and his sun came out. "Even though."

Madison came around the circle and waved. "Hi, Uncle Sheriff."

"Hey, squirt. Looking good up there."

"Dallas is an awesome teacher." She patted the

side of the horse's neck. "So is Sadie. I love her so much."

Horse and rider circled on past as Lawson and Dallas exchanged looks.

"Enthusiasm," he said. "I like it."

"And a smile," Dallas said. "She's making huge strides."

"Thanks to you."

"Not just me. She needs you, Lawson. Cares about you too, and she's starting not to be so afraid of showing it."

"Underneath the gruff exterior, she's a good kid. She's been reading the devotional the Sunday school teacher gave her. She asked me some questions about it."

"Me too," Dallas said.

"More progress. Speaking of which, have you thought any more about our local radio station?" His pulse thrummed while he awaited her answer.

"They offered me a position, a morning show playing music and making small talk with the commuters."

"What did you say?" He wanted so badly for her to say yes.

She shrugged a shoulder. "It's a job, and I need one."

Not exactly the level of enthusiasm he'd hoped for.

"Will you be happy there? Is it what you want?" He prayed it was, but he wouldn't push. She had to want this for herself.

A tiny frown marred her forehead. "I don't know. Maybe it would work for now until the Aaron episode blows over."

And then she'd head back to the big city. Lawson's chest ached with the knowledge that her feelings for him didn't run as deep as his for her.

"Calypso would be lucky to have you, but you need to do what's best for you. Whatever that might be." Even if it killed him to keep his mouth shut and his love inside.

She turned to squeeze his arm. "Thank you. Your encouragement means a lot."

Madison circled again, stopping this time next to the fence. "Are you guys going to ride?"

Dallas nodded. "Sure, if your uncle wants to. I won't get to do this in Bayville."

Right. Bayville. Where she lived. Where she wanted to be.

To cover his emotions, he climbed over the railings and walked up to Madison and the horse. "You really like this mare, don't you?"

"Love her. She's so sweet."

"Even if she's losing her sight?"

Madison's face clouded up. "Even more then. I'd take care of her forever if you'd let me."

"Would you like to have her? As your own."

"For real?" She frowned, suspicious, a fact that pierced his heart.

Lawson stroked the dependable old muzzle. "For real. She's yours as long as you're willing to take care of her."

Madison tossed her ponytail, but her gleam of joy was unmistakable. "That's, like, forever and always."

He felt Dallas come up beside him and glanced her way. She was looking at him as if he were her hero.

"Did you hear that, Dallas?" Madison asked. "Sadie's mine now forever."

"I heard. A horse is a big responsibility, but I think you're up for it."

"I am. I promise." She clicked her tongue, and the mare plodded slowly forward. "Oh, Sadie, aren't you happy? You're mine. You and me. Forever and ever."

Dallas hooked her arm in Lawson's elbow as they watched the girl and her horse. "That was a wonderful thing to do."

"Sadie needs a keeper. Madison needs a horse."

LINDA GOODNIGHT

"Sadie's not the only one who's happy."

"Good to see Madison this way." He worried about her most of the time, questioned himself the rest. Was he doing the right things? Was this what a good father would do? Not that Madison had ever experienced a doting dad. "Do you think she's settling in?"

"I do. Progress is slow but faster than I expected. You're a good uncle."

"I'm starting to like the way that feels."

"And that surprises you?"

"It does. Me, a too-busy bachelor with a cranky teenage niece? It feels strange, but I actually look forward to coming home to her every night." Hand covering hers, he walked them back to the fence. "You might have something to do with that too."

"Oh, yeah?" She tilted her head, flirting.

Every male blood cell reacted. "Yeah."

He leaned in to kiss her just as his cell phone vibrated against his shirt pocket.

With a sigh and a wry shake of his head, Lawson said, "Hold that thought."

Her chuckle was throaty and warm. "My pleasure."

"Sheriff Hawk," he said into the receiver. And then, "What do you want now?"

As he listened, his mood plummeted.

"No," he said when he could get a word in edge-ways. "Not a good plan." Or good timing. Before the caller could say more, Lawson hung up.

He stared across the corral toward his niece and her beloved Sadie, still moving round and round the lot, Madison's smile big enough to break his heart. He had some serious thinking to do. And fast.

A soft hand touched him. "Is everything okay?"

"No. It's not." His terse tone brought her around in front of him.

"Anything I can do?"

"I don't know." He perched a hand on each hip, watching Madison approach, wondering about the right thing to do. "That was Bryce."

"Madison's dad?"

"The one and only." The words tasted bitter. "He wants me to ship her to Nashville. Like some package of junk he left behind."

"Oh, Lawson. What are you going to do?" Dallas followed his gaze to the young rider.

"He's her father. I'm not." Even if he was starting to want to be.

"But she's stable and thriving here. From our conversations, I know she wasn't either one with her father. Not even close."

He'd gathered the same sad understanding. Bryce had dragged her all over the country in pursuit of one pipedream after another, leaving her alone as often as he was with her. "Yeah, the situation stinks, but I don't really have a choice."

"Does he have a good place for them to live? Will she be alone all the time the way she was before?"

"I don't know." Lawson's tight jaw flexed. "First time he's called since she arrived. And you know what? He didn't even ask about her or ask to speak to her. Just told me to ship her. His words."

Dallas remembered what Madison had angrily told her. Kids don't have a choice. "She's hinted to me that she wants to stay with you. Shouldn't her opinion count?"

"It counts with me." He raked a hand over his hair. "I don't know, Dallas. Bryce is so irresponsible, he may change his mind tomorrow. Or send her back here a month from now. That's been his entire life, and Madison's too."

"The reasons she's confused and distrustful."

His gaze flashed to the oncoming rider. "I have to tell her."

"Now? When she's still basking in the glow of Sadie?"

"You think she'll be upset?"

"I do. Even though she misses her dad and would love for him to call her once in a while, she's smart. She knows life with him is inconsistent and lonely. Did you know she's attended fourteen schools already?"

Lawson groaned and shook his head. "Maybe I should talk to Bryce again first. See what's going on with him before I tell her."

"That's a good idea."

He extracted the phone from his pocket. "Keep her occupied, would you, please?"

And he walked inside the barn.

Five minutes later, he walked back out, phone in hand.

"Madison," he called. "Your dad wants to talk to you."

"My dad? Really?" The girl gently turned the reins and rode to her uncle. After sliding from the saddle, she took the outstretched cell, her eyes wide and questioning. Wary, too. "Dad?"

Dallas clasped Lawson's hand and backed away to give Madison some privacy.

They'd barely moved when Madison yelled. "No way! I'm not doing that anymore, and you can't make me. I'll run away again."

Dallas exchanged a look with Lawson.

"Again?" he mouthed.

The exchange continued for another few minutes before Madison returned the phone to Lawson.

"He wants to talk to you." Face red, expression furious, she said, "If you don't want me here, fine. But I'm not going to Nashville to be his maid."

She whirled and stormed toward the house.

Dallas sprang into action. "Madison, wait."

The teen stopped but didn't turn. Was she crying?

Approaching with caution and a prayer to say the right thing, Dallas stepped in front of Madison.

Quietly, she asked, "Didn't you forget something?"

"What?" Madison bit out the words, the tears she refused to shed trembling on her eyelashes.

Dallas slid a long look at the mare. Sadie stood quietly waiting beside the fence, still saddled.

"Oh." Madison softened, then crossed her arms and glanced away. "I won't be here to take care of her anyway."

Her voice throbbed with grief.

Aching for the girl, Dallas tenderly smoothed the fine, stray hairs away from Madison's face. "No matter how this turns out, Sadie's depending on you *now*. She trusts you."

A single tear sprang loose. "Uncle Sheriff said I

could have her. Now, I can't. He'll make me go to Nashville. And who could blame him?"

"You think Lawson wants you to leave?"

"He never wanted me in the first place. He was just too Dudley Do-Right to dump me the way my dad does."

The pain of rejection was so strong, Dallas felt it in her own heart. "I think you're wrong about that."

"Trust me. I know what a prize I am. He'll send me, and he won't even regret the ticket money." She hissed out a derisive sound. "Who cares? I never wanted to come to this stupid town in the first place."

Dallas saw through the bravado. Madison denied she cared to cover up exactly how much she did.

"Do you, or do you not, want to remain here on the ranch with your uncle and Sadie?"

Madison's shoulder's jerked. "Don't know, don't care, doesn't matter."

"Yes, it does. It matters to you, to me, to Lawson. To Sadie, too. Be honest. If you could choose, would you stay?"

"Maybe." Madison sniffed and tossed her pony tail. "If he wants me to. I mean, I could be a lot of help to him. But if Dad wants me in Nashville…"

The child was clearly torn between the life she longed for and her responsibility to her father.

"Let's you and I take care of Sadie. She's your responsibility now. We'll worry about the rest later." Dallas offered a turned-up hand. "Okay?"

Madison gently slapped the palm with hers. "Okay."

They headed toward the corral and led the mare inside the barn. Lawson, Dallas noted, was still talking on the phone. When he saw them coming, he turned and walked toward the pasture. Dallas got the message. Madison didn't need to hear what was said between the half-brothers.

Before they'd finished grooming the mare, Lawson joined them in the barn. The phone was in his shirt pocket.

Busy brushing the horse, Madison stopped when she saw her uncle.

Lawson had on his professional face. "Your dad says you can stay."

Resuming Sadie's grooming, Madison pretended not to care, but before she lowered her eyes, Dallas saw a flare of hope. "You don't have to keep me if you don't want to. I got places to go."

"What if I want to?"

Madison huffed. "Then you'd be crazier than my dad."

"Always have been."

The brush stalled. Madison's head jerked up. "So I'm staying?"

"You're staying."

"Okay. Cool." Madison pushed her face into the mare's mane, but not before Dallas saw the smile.

CHAPTER 11

"*H*ow did you get Bryce to agree?" Dallas asked Lawson hours later after a bouncy Madison retired to her room.

The two of them were sitting side by side on Lawson's western-style couch, feet propped on the coffee table. Both had shed their shoes at the door.

"It wasn't hard, I'm sorry to say." He kept his voice low in case Madison was listening. "My brother doesn't like responsibility. Once I explained that she was doing well here, and that I was willing to keep her, he was eager to say yes. The thousand bucks I promised him didn't hurt either."

Dallas squeaked. "You're giving him money so you can raise his child?"

"Don't make it sound illegal. Bryce is broke, as

always, and the money is a loan. As long as he calls or emails her once a week and let's her live here until graduation, he doesn't have to repay it."

What kind of man would do what Lawson had? But Dallas knew. A good one. A man with a big heart and a powerful sense of family responsibility.

"You law dogs are sneaky creatures."

"A man does what a man has to do. And Madison seemed okay with spending a few years with her mean old Uncle Sheriff."

"She's ecstatic, Lawson. You should have heard some of the things she said to me while you were changing. She's already making plans for the junior prom."

Lawson touched a hand to his chest and grimaced. "Spare me the dating game."

"It will happen."

"I know, but let her be in love with horses for a while longer before I have to deal with boys."

"She's always going to love horses. I can see it in her eyes."

He started to rise. "Want some tea or something?"

She waved him off. "No. I'm good. Sit back down and relax. You've had an interesting day."

"So have you. How was your shopping trip with your sister?"

"I still get a jolt when I hear those words. Do you know how often I've wished for a sister?"

"And Emily will be a good one."

"She's great. I already love her." Dallas tipped her head back, lifting her hair off her neck. It seemed she'd known Emily forever, as if their shared genetics bonded them somehow. Maybe they did. "We had a blast trying on everything in sight, laughing at the way we looked in some of the new styles, and just hanging out together. I spent money I shouldn't have, but it's good to have some different clothes to wear."

"You always look perfect to me."

Her pulse jittered. It was doing that a lot lately, and the reaction had nothing to do with migraines. She cared for Lawson. Maybe more than cared.

Considering her situation, was that a good thing?

"If I take the job at the local station, I'll need to make a trip to Bayville for my other belongings and decide what to do about my condo." The lease wasn't up for another few months.

The lawman's face brightened. "Let me know in advance so I can take off work and tag along. You might need some muscle."

"I might." She also loved the idea of driving eight hours with Lawson to anywhere. If she stayed in

Calypso for a while, she could spend all the time she wanted with him.

Dallas reached for his hand. The position at Calypso Radio sounded better all the time.

GOOD WEATHER BROUGHT out the crazies.

This was Lawson's thought days later as the paperwork piled up on his desk inside the courthouse. He and his deputies, as well as the city police officers, had been too busy to take a breath for three solid days. Add the meetings he was supposed to attend and the budget he needed to tweak, and he was up to his eyeballs.

He'd even had to short-circuit his free time with Dallas and Madison to work on reports. He hadn't been a bit happy about that, although knowing Dallas was on his ranch every evening helped a little. At least, his niece didn't have to be alone while he slaved over paperwork.

Dallas had even offered to teach Madison to barrel race. Which meant, he'd have to buy and train another horse. Sadie sure couldn't run the barrels. But it also meant Dallas was serious about taking the position at Calypso radio, so he figured another horse was money well spent.

"Sheriff?" Deputy Shell stepped through the doorway. "Got some reports for you to sign."

Lawson groaned. "More?"

"Sorry. It's wild this week." Ronnie set the paperwork on the desk and backed toward the exit.

After giving the departing deputy and the papers a scathing glare, Lawson rubbed his burning eyes and returned his attention to the computer screen and the budget that didn't want to balance. The numbers began to swim. Maybe he needed glasses. Either that, or he'd been at this too long.

To preserve his ego, Lawson decided on the later, pushed away from the desk and went to the coffee maker. It was empty.

Growling like a dog at whomever emptied and didn't refill, Lawson yanked the carafe from the stand.

His office door opened. He whipped around, ready to grouse about any more paperwork.

His bad mood and fatigue disappeared. He got that swooping feeling in his belly that happened every time Dallas came within his radar.

"You're a much needed interruption. Come in. Convince me to quit my job."

She smiled. "You love this job."

Yeah. And I love you, too. How about that for a kick in the head?

Of course, he didn't voice those thoughts. It was too soon and their relationship—or progress thereof —still hinged on her career choices.

"Rough week." He put the carafe back on the stand and decided to forget the coffee.

"I noticed. You're working long hours."

"Nature of the business. It ebbs and flows. Some weeks are nuts. Others are slow." He swept a hand toward a chair. "Sit. Tell me why a beautiful woman like you is in the sheriff's office. Did you commit another crime?"

Dallas laughed, a sound he was growing fond of, and held out her joined wrists. "Will you arrest me?"

"Not if it means filling out another report."

"Oh, good. I robbed a bank and stashed the money in an offshore account. Want to run away to Tahiti with me?"

He chuckled, as she'd intended, although running away with her sounded very promising. "Don't confess. There's paperwork involved."

She leaned toward him, and her warm, classy fragrance floated across the desk. "I have some exciting news."

"You took the job?" Please, please, let her say yes.

"Yes. But not the one in Calypso."

His heart tumbled. "Where?"

"Bayville. My old boss called about an hour ago. Ratings are down. Advertisers are over their fear. I'm no longer a pariah. They want me back." Her eyes sparkled, and she looked animated enough to dance around the room.

Lawson's world, the world he'd been dreaming of since meeting Dallas, came crashing down. He schooled his features, a trick of his trade. Never let the emotions show.

"You're sure this is what you want? After the way they treated you before?"

"It is. Oh, Lawson, I'm beside myself with excitement. I can't believe they asked me back, with a raise!"

"I can. They came to their senses and realized what a treasure you are." The burning in his eyes grew worse. He needed glasses for sure. "So, when do you head to Bayville?"

"Probably tomorrow. Maybe the next day. Not sure yet. I want to say goodbye to my siblings and, of course, to Madison."

"Of course." He wasn't sure he could live through another evening in her company knowing she would leave. Knowing she didn't care enough to stay.

But he would do it for her. He was that crazy. And it had been that kind of week.

TWO DAYS LATER, Lawson stood next to Dallas's little red SUV outside the Royal Bed and Breakfast. Madison had insisted on coming along, and she stood next to him, looking as glum as he felt.

"You'll call me, won't you?" Madison said to Dallas.

"Yes, and you can call me. Anytime. And remember, I'll be back. I have family here now."

"Right."

Madison looked about as impressed with that statement as he was. He loved that Dallas had a reason to return. Selfishly, he wanted that reason to be him.

She slammed the back door of her vehicle and hugged Madison. Then she turned to him.

What was he supposed to do? Kiss her? Wish her good luck and God speed? Pretend he wasn't dying inside or entertaining insane notions about abduction?

She saved him the decision when she put her arms over his shoulders and tugged him down to her level.

"Thank you for everything," she whispered, her warm breath tickling his lips and making him too aware of all he'd miss once she was gone. "I'll miss you."

"Me too." The thought of how much nearly choked off his air. Somehow, he remained calm. Somehow, he managed not to beg or whimper. "It's been special. You're special."

She touched his cheek. "So are you."

For the last time, he kissed her, a bittersweet, tender, lingering kiss that seared him all the way through.

Dallas pulled away first, her eyes holding his.

She seemed to hesitate then, as if she weren't sure, as if she had more to say, but the uncertainty disappeared as fast it had come. She was leaving, and there was nothing he could do but be a man about it.

"You take care now. You hear?" he said and turned her toward the car.

"You too. I'll call you when I get home."

"You do that."

She started the car, and he shut the door, the snick sounding with too much finality. He pecked on the window. She rolled it down.

"Drive safely. If you have any trouble, call a cop.

Me." He managed a crooked grin. "And watch your speed. The sheriff in this town is a real stickler."

His words had the desired effect. Her smile bloomed. "Bye, Lawson."

The window slid up. And then the little red SUV pulled away from the bed and breakfast…and out of his life.

"This stinks." Madison slammed the kitchen cabinet door hard enough to rattle the dishes. They'd just finished a dinner that neither of them had the appetite for. "Why'd she have to get that stupid job back, anyway?"

"She has a life elsewhere, Madison. We knew she'd leave sooner or later."

"But she was gonna teach me to barrel race."

"I can do that."

"It's not the same." She put a glass on the shelf. "No offense."

"I hear you."

They were in this boat together, he and Madison. Funny how losing Dallas had bonded them. For the past two weeks, they'd moped and consoled each other. Eventually, Madison would wander out to the barn and not return until bedtime. Lawson would work on reports or watch basketball and try to ignore the hot, empty place in his chest.

He washed the last dish and handed it to her. "Are you keeping up with school?"

"Yeah. It's easy." She stuck a towel in the glass and twisted it. "You miss her a lot, don't you?"

Enough that he'd driven to the top of Wolf Hill last night, the highest spot in Calypso, and tried for more than an hour to pick up KVXN on his radio. No luck. Bayville was too far away.

Today, he'd bought a candle that smelled like her perfume.

"Can't deny it," he said.

"You in love with her or something?"

"Doesn't matter now, does it?"

She hitched out an annoyed teenager sound. "Adults can be so dense. If you love her, you should go after her and tell her. Bring her home."

Home. "She is home."

"You should still tell her. I mean, wouldn't you want to know if she was in love with you?"

And there lay the dilemma. "When you love someone, Maddy, you want the best for them. You want them to be happy."

"So you make yourself unhappy? That's dumb."

"Who says I'm unhappy. I love my ranch and my

town and my job." He tossed a dish towel at her, hoping to break off this painful conversation. "And you."

Catching the towel against her shirt, Madison said, "She liked us. I know she did."

"She did, especially you."

Madison did the eye roll thing. This time, he thought it was cute. "Dallas was so into you, it gagged me sometimes."

"Yeah. Well, liking isn't love. Just remember that when you start dating."

"When can I?" Her attention was finally diverted.

Lawson pulled a horrified face. "Never."

Madison giggled. A real honest to goodness little-girl giggle. She'd never done that before.

And Lawson realized something. Even though Madison was disappointed to see Dallas leave town, she was happy here with him.

And he decided to let that make him happy too.

One happy lady was better than none.

CHAPTER 12

"Good show, Dallas."

"Thanks, Jay." Her boss was waiting in the hallway as she exited the on-air booth.

"KVXN missed you. It's sure great to have you back."

"Thanks."

Dallas pressed a hand to the nape of her neck. She was tired. Returning to the grind of a nightly show proved exhausting when, in the past, the hours behind the microphone, chatting up strangers, had energized her.

"Everything okay?" Jay frowned in concern. "Not getting one of your headaches, are you?"

Maybe that was the problem. An impending migraine. Sometimes they stirred around in her head for a few days before erupting. "I'm fine. Just need to take my medication."

His beefy hand patted her shoulder in a brotherly manner. "You do that. And get some rest."

"Will do."

After stopping in the office for her handbag, she headed home to her condo.

When she arrived, the windows of her house were dark. She was alone. She should be accustomed to that, but the place seemed empty and lonely. She missed the glowing welcome at Lawson's ranch. She missed sharing her day with him and Madison and hearing about theirs. She missed propping her bare feet next to Lawson's sock footed ones and snuggling on his couch while Madison rolled her eyes and made gagging sounds.

Inside the condo, she tossed her bag on a chair and went to the sink for her medication.

Given the brief time she'd spent in Calypso, she didn't understand this empty feeling, but she couldn't shake it. All she'd wanted was to get her job back and to move on from Aaron's tragedy. Yet, here she was, every night, thinking about Lawson. Wanting to call him but resisting. If she heard his voice, she might—

Downing the pills, she chased them with water.

She might what? Tell him she loved him?

She collapsed on the couch and closed her eyes. Her career was important. She was going places, climbing the ladder.

Could love happen that fast? Did Lawson feel the same?

Pressing a hand to her forehead, she tried to pray. All she saw behind her eyelids was Lawson's face.

When had she become so confused?

The doorbell rang. Dallas sat up. The hour was late for most people, but her best friend Bethany knew Dallas liked to wind down for an hour or so after work. Sometimes she'd come over with a pint of rocky road. Ice cream sounded really good right now.

Grateful for the interruption to her ping-ponging thoughts, Dallas went to answer. Squinting one eye, she peeked through the peephole. Her stomach leaped. She yanked the door open.

"Madison!"

"Miss me?" The girl walked right in, unloading her backpack on the living room floor. "Nice place."

Dallas looked outside, saw no one else, and shut the door. "What are you doing here? Is Lawson with you?"

Her stomach clenched in hope.

"No. Just me, myself and I. Aren't you absolutely de-lighted?"

She was. She was also taken aback. "How did you get here?"

"I hitched. But don't panic." Madison flopped in a chair and spread out both arms. "I'm safe, as you can see."

Alarm prickled the hairs on her arms. "You hitch-hiked from Calypso to Bayville?" Of all the foolish things to do, and for what reason? "Didn't Lawson tell you to never again to get in a vehicle with a stranger?"

"I don't plan on making it a habit." All teenage confidence and audacity, Madison yawned and stretched. "Not anymore, anyway. The last guy was kind of creepy."

"Oh, my goodness." Dallas wilted onto the couch again, this time with her eyes wide open. "What happened?"

"Nothing serious. But he kept asking me if I was alone, and he had this funny look in his eyes. Kind of smarmy, like I was an ice cream cone. He even asked if I liked older guys." She stuck her tongue out and pretended to gag. "Can you imagine?"

The migraine was coming on fast. Dallas rubbed her temples. Madison had no concept of the danger she'd put herself in. She was too young, too vulnerable, and far too pretty. This hitchhiking insanity had to stop.

"I finally told the dude that my dad was meeting me, and he was a cop." Madison snickered at her ingenuity. "That shut him up. After that, he couldn't wait to get me out of the truck. Kind of handy to have a cop uncle."

"You can't ever do that again." Dallas used her sternest voice. "Ever. You hear me?"

"Sure." Madison jerked a nonchalant shoulder. "I hear you."

She heard, but would she follow through? "I mean it. If anything happened to you..."

The cocky expression left the girl's face. "You'd care, wouldn't you? You really would."

"I'd be devastated. So would your uncle." Dallas sat up, wishing the medication would kick in. Her thinking was getting wacky. "What's this all about, Madison? Does Lawson know you're here?"

"Probably by now. I left a note on the fridge."

"You need to call him. He's probably frantic with worry."

Madison held up a stop-sign hand. "Not yet. Not until you and me have a little talk."

"About what?"

"You and Uncle Sheriff." Suddenly serious, the girl leaned forward, clasped hands pressed between her knees. "I thought you should know. He misses you real bad. He mopes around like a sick puppy. Love sick, if you get my drift."

Dallas pressed her fingertips against her mouth. Lawson had never said a word about love. Was Madison telling the truth? "He told you this?"

"Yep. Sure did. I twisted his arm a little, but he finally admitted it. He's crazy about you. It would be sweet if he wasn't so pathetic. So I came to ask. Do you love him back? 'Cause if you do, you can drive me home and put him out of his misery."

A disbelieving laugh spurted from Dallas. The outrageous imp. "I have a job here, Madison. I can't just get up and leave." Even if she wanted to. "Besides, your uncle is a grown man. If he has something to say to me, he'll handle it on his own."

"No, he won't. He has this dumb idea about wanting you to be happy." Madison made a sound of disgust. "That part's not dumb, but he thinks he has to be unhappy so that you're not."

"You do realize how little sense that makes."

"That's what I told him!" Madison slapped both hands against the chair arms. "So, do you love him or not? I really need to know."

"Love isn't that simple."

Madison groaned, eyes toward the ceiling. "Adults are so dumb. Yes or no seems pretty simple to me."

"All right. Yes. I do love him." Tears pushed at the back of her eyelids. No wonder she was miserable in Bayville. The lonely, empty ache inside was for Lawson. He was the reason *Dallas after Dark* no longer fulfilled her. She missed him, needed him in her life, wanted him. *Loved* him.

Madison beamed. "There you go. That wasn't so hard, was it?"

"But I think you're wrong about your uncle. He misses me, of course. We had a great time together. But love? No." Madison, with her desperate need for family, had let her teenage imagination run amok. "Lawson is a confirmed bachelor, too busy to settle down." He'd said as much. He'd even encouraged her to take the Bayville job without a hint that he wanted her to remain in Calypso. Not a single hint. And that had hurt. A lot.

The dratted tears threatened again. She batted them away.

For the first time, Madison's confidence wavered. She looked like what she was-a young, needy kid. "Don't you miss us at all?"

"Very much." Too much, as in desperately. She rummaged in her purse and handed over her phone. "Call him, Madison."

"Do you want me to give him a message from you? Something romantic and mushy?"

"No, I do not." She had a lot of thinking to do, but first things first. "Call him before he has every cop in America looking for you."

"Oh, gosh. I never thought of that." Madison pushed up from the chair and looked around. "Where's the bathroom? I gotta go."

"Straight down the hall on the left. Are you hungry?"

"Starving."

Probably hadn't eaten all day. "You make the call. I'll make the sandwich." And then try to figure out what to do from here.

"Mayo, not mustard."

"I remember."

Madison blinked. "You do?"

'It hasn't been that long."

"It has been to us."

And while Dallas absorbed that sweet statement, Madison disappeared down the hall.

. . .

LAWSON WASN'T prone to panic. He was a peace officer, for crying out loud, trained to remain calm in the worst of circumstances.

But nothing had trained him for dealing with a recalcitrant niece. A niece he was responsible for. A niece he'd come to love, attitude and all.

He read the note again. "Don't worry. I'll fix things." She'd signed it with x's and o's and a big, swooping M.

Fix what? The problems with her dad? But they were already fixed.

Surely, she didn't mean the situation with Dallas. That was a done deal. Dallas was gone for good. The best he could hope for was an occasional visit.

He slapped the note on the table. He had no idea when she'd left or how long she'd been gone. Work had kept him much later than usual today. He'd known it would, so he'd told Madison last night to ride the school bus home. If she'd skipped school—and he wouldn't put it past her—she could be in Nashville by now.

He'd given her some money. Had she bought a bus ticket?

"Please, God," he prayed, "not hitchhiking." But that's exactly the kind of thing Madison would do.

Where had she gone? And why hadn't he bought her the cell phone she'd wanted?

Frantic with worry, he called Jenny first. Her friend confirmed his fears. Madison hadn't been at school, but Jenny didn't know why.

He started to call Dallas but resisted. If Madison wasn't there, Dallas would worry, and there was nothing she could do to help.

Lawson sure wasn't calling Bryce, who'd accuse him of losing his kid. Which he had, in a manner of speaking, but that was beside the point.

The only thing left to do was to report her missing and put his law enforcement buddies on the look-out.

His phone vibrated in his hand. Dallas's number glowed like a beacon.

"Dallas?" He said into the phone before the caller could speak. "Have you heard from Madison?"

There was a pause and then a girlish voice. "Uncle Sheriff. It's me. Madison."

His eyes fell shut. *Thank you, God.*

All Lawson's adrenaline drained to the floor. He leaned against a wall, weak as a baby. "Where are you? Are you okay? What are you doing?"

"I'm okay, but I'm with Dallas in Bayville, and she's not okay. She's sick."

The adrenaline shot back up. "What's wrong? Is it a migraine?"

"Something bad. You need to come here right now."

It was eight hours to Bayville. He was too far away to help. "If she's in distress, call 9-1-1. I can't get there fast enough."

"Oh, shoot, I didn't think about that."

The offhanded remark sent his suspicious cop-antenna straight up. "What's going on? Is there something you're not telling me? Let me speak to Dallas."

"No! I mean..." She gave an exasperated huff. "Okay, here's the real story. You need to come here because Dallas misses us and she loves us and she thinks you don't. And I'm sure you can fix it if you'll just come and talk to her."

Oh, boy, a misguided teenage matchmaker.

"Did she tell you all this?"

"Would I make up something like that?" A tiny chuckle. "Okay, I probably would, but I didn't. I promise. I told her your dumb idea about making her happy or whatever and she got all teary-eyed. She thought you didn't want her."

"Why would she think that?" He wanted her more than his next breath. If he had one inkling that she felt the same, he'd walk to Bayville. Barefoot. On glass.

"Because you didn't ask her to stay. You told her to take the dumb job."

He had. "It was what she wanted." Wasn't it? Had he missed the signals? Had she been waiting for him to ask her to stay?

"I want her back." Madison's voice was low and achy. "Don't you?"

Lawson gripped the phone like a lifeline. "I do, but that's adult business, Madison. Between me and Dallas."

He couldn't believe he was having this conversation with a thirteen-year-old.

"But I have this great idea."

"Whoa. Stop. Is Dallas really sick?"

"Not exactly. I kind of made that up. But she *is* lying on the couch, and she *was* rubbing her head. That part's true."

"Could be a migraine. Or a pain-in-the-neck teenager."

Madison snickered. "I'll look out for her until you get here."

Lawson growled into the phone. "You'd better."

"Ugh. Does that mean I'm grounded or something?"

"Without a doubt, but we'll talk about that in person."

"So, you're coming?" The excitement in her voice was palpable.

"How else would you get back to Calypso? And don't say, hitchhike."

"I promised Dallas I wouldn't, but if you don't come to Bayville…"

"I'm coming," he growled. "You stay put. Don't even go outside until I get there. Now, put Dallas on the phone."

CHAPTER 13

$\mathcal{M}$adison came into the kitchen, grinning, the phone outstretched. "He wants to talk to you."

Dallas's heart leaped. With Madison's tale about Lawson's confessions of love running through her mind, she felt almost too shy to answer. And she'd never had a shy bone in her body.

Taking the phone, she turned her back, leaving the hungry teen to wolf down the sandwich and a tall glass of milk.

"Hello."

"Dallas." His voice was tense. "Are you sick?"

Oh, that wonderful, manly voice. Pleasant chills danced over her skin.

215

"No. Why?" And why had he asked about her first instead of his niece?

"Madison thought you might be getting a migraine."

She made a humming sound. "She could cause one."

"Or a heart attack. I think I had two today."

Dallas huffed into the phone. "Can you believe she pulled such a stunt?"

"Unfortunately, I can. But I'm relieved to know she's safe with someone I trust, someone she loves."

"Me, too. Anything could have happened. Being in law enforcement, you know that better than I."

"I don't even want to think about it. I've tried scare tactics, but getting the dangers through her thick head is like trying to make Bryce act responsibly. She thinks she's indestructible."

"She's too street smart for her own good, even if her heart was in the right place. You know why she's here, don't you?" Dallas held her breath, waiting for his reply.

"Now I do, and I'm sorry about that, too. She shouldn't intrude in adult business. It's a little embarrassing."

Sorry? As in, sorry Madison had blurted out

something he hadn't been ready to share? Or sorry he hadn't talked to her himself?

"Don't apologize, Lawson. I was glad to see her, even under the circumstances." And I was thrilled to hear what she had to say. If she was telling the truth.

"Little alien does get under your skin, doesn't she?"

"So does someone else."

"Yeah?"

In for a penny, in for a pound. "I miss you, Lawson."

"That's good to hear. I miss you too." Was that longing in his voice? "But your work is every bit as important to you as mine is to me." A slight pause as if he were choosing his words carefully. "It'll be good to see you tomorrow."

Meaning exactly what? That he loved her and couldn't wait to get here? Or was he only being his usual, nice self? "You're driving down here?"

"As long as you don't mind if Madison spends tonight at your place."

Mind? She was ecstatic. Tomorrow, Lawson would be here, in Bayville. With her. "She'll be good company."

"Thank you."

They were quiet for a moment, each content to

know the other was listening. The way they'd been since the beginning. Comfortable together. Dallas felt the connection from his heart to hers through the wireless lines.

The emptiness of earlier seemed to fade, along with the warnings in the back of her head.

"My headache's going away," she said. "It must have needed to hear your voice."

"Guess that means I'm good medicine."

"I could use another dose."

He laughed, and the sound filled her up like a hot air balloon.

Reluctant to end the conversation, she pivoted, went to the window overlooking the parking lot, and pushed aside the drapes. "How's everything in Calypso County?"

"Busy. A little lonely."

"Same here."

"How's the show going?"

"Great." *She* wasn't great, but the show was. "The station owners are pleased, ad revenues are up, and my callers are interesting, as always."

"So, you're glad to be back in the saddle?"

How did she answer that question? She settled for the truth. "It isn't as satisfying as it once was."

His voice lowered, rumbled, when he asked, "Why is that?"

Might as well say it. "You're not here."

A short chuckle. "I understand. My job is great, but since you left...I don't know how to describe it."

"Lonely? Empty?"

"That's about the size of it."

Joy bloomed in Dallas's chest. "Me, too."

"Can we talk about this more tomorrow? In person."

"About us?"

"Yes. You. Me. Us."

"I'd like that very much."

Lawson sighed, a long, relieved sound. He loved her. She could hear it in that sigh.

And for tonight, that was enough.

THE NEXT MORNING, Dallas dressed and went into the kitchen for a yogurt and juice, wondering how she'd get through the hours before Lawson arrived. What would she say to him? Should she spill her heart and hope for the best?

Madison, like any self-respecting teenager, was still sound asleep. After yesterday's long trip, she'd probably wouldn't regain consciousness until noon.

Dallas's cell phone chimed and, hoping it was Lawson, she grabbed it from the counter. The text was from Emily, asking when she'd be back in Calypso. The Caldwell brood already missed her.

Yesterday, it had been Wyatt. The day before Connie, and she'd talked on the phone several times to each one.

She was falling in love with her father's family, and she still hadn't told her mother about them.

After shooting back a text promising to visit soon, she put a pod in the coffee machine and, feeling guilty for keeping the secret, texted an "I love you" to her mother.

As the coffee gurgled to a stop, the doorbell rang. Four times in rapid succession.

Who on earth?

She opened the door to a cowboy with a scruffy, unshaven face and very red eyes. He looked exhausted…and gorgeous.

Before she could think of any reason why she shouldn't, she jumped into his arms and kissed him.

"Good morning to you, too." His words rumbled against her lips.

Dallas backed away, but not too far. Just far enough to see his deep fatigue. "You must have driven all night! Are you crazy? Oh, it's so good to see you!"

"Wow. Madison must have been a terror." He looked a little dazed, but in a delighted way.

"She was perfect. And still sleeping." Dallas tugged her cowboy sheriff into the condo and shut the door, wishing to be back in his arms. She was making a fool of herself. She had to stop. Calm down. But it was marvelous to see him. Did he feel the same?

Getting a firm rein on herself, she said, "Want some coffee."

"No. I want more of this." With a hand to either cheek, Lawson pulled her face up close, grinned into her eyes, and kissed her until they both trembled.

When he finally stopped, she wilted against him. His heart thundered beneath her ear.

"I think you really did miss me," she said.

"More than missed you."

She raised her head to look into his eyes. What she saw made her pulse stutter. "How so?"

He drew in a breath, let it out. "I realize your career is everything to you, and I won't pressure you, but a certain nosey teenager convinced me that you had a right to know my feelings. What you do with them is up to you. Okay?"

"Okay. I think." She dropped her head to one side and frowned. "Exactly, what are you trying to say?

Something fierce and lovely blazed in his eyes. "I'm crazy in love with you, Dallas. Never planned it, never expected it, never thought I'd ever feel this way, but there it is. If I had my wishes, you'd go back to Calypso with me today and never leave again."

"I can't today."

His wonderful face, full of hope, fell. "Right. I understand."

Heart soaring, she cupped his whiskered cheek. "I don't think you do. I can't leave today. But soon, after I give my notice at the station and take care of business here in Bayville."

His lips parted. "You mean it?"

She nodded, so happy she could barely breathe. This was what she'd longed for. This was what she truly wanted. Lawson and his love.

"I'm crazy in love with you, too," she said, marveling, "and I didn't even know it."

"But your career…"

"Is important to me, yes. But, if they still want me, I can create a new and even better show in Calypso. Close to you. Close to my new family."

He dragged a weary hand down his face. The

whiskery sound scraped the air. "Man. I must have fallen asleep at the wheel. This has to be a dream."

"If it is, I'm having it too." She looped her arms around his neck. "Don't wake me up."

"This is my dream, so I'm saying it again. I love you, Dallas Langley." He kissed her. "Now, it's your turn."

"I love you, Lawson Hawk." And she kissed him, this time with enough power to make his knees weak.

"You can do that a million times if you want to. Since it's my dream and all."

In between, I love yous, she did.

She was nearly to twenty of those million kisses —these things took time—when she heard a door open. Footsteps echoed in the hallway.

"Madison's up," she whispered.

They should probably break apart, but Dallas couldn't bring herself to move. Not now. Not when she finally knew he loved her, and she loved him. The moment was too special, too new, and too marvelous to let go.

In a moment, the teenager appeared in the doorway, pants and T-shirt baggy, hair sticking up like quills on a porcupine.

With her usual disgust, Madison cocked a hand

on one hip and grumbled, "Could you two hold it down, please? People are trying to sleep around here."

She started to turn but stopped and did a double take at the scene before her, her eyes widening as she came more awake. Dallas clinging to Lawson. His arms tightly around her. Both of them probably with stars in their eyes.

"Well. It's about time." She sniffed. "Carry on."

Then, grinning like the famous cat, she headed back to bed.

Lawson laughed against Dallas's hair. "Carry on. I like the sound of that."

"Me, too." She turned her lips up toward his. "I think I was at twenty-one."

"Better start all over to be sure."

And, with a joyous laugh, Dallas did exactly that.

aylight with Dallas was the new buzz term in Calypso and all across eastern Texas. The popular morning show, hosted by Dallas Langley, had rocketed to the top, drawing more listeners than larger competitors. Everyone credited Dallas's rich dulcet voice and her unique blend of psychology, music, common sense and a genuine respectful love of her listeners for the program's startling success.

Lawson couldn't be prouder or more delighted for his lady love. In the six months since she'd moved to Calypso and taken over the morning show, their love had matured and deepened. He'd never before considered marriage. Now he did.

"Think she suspects anything?" Wyatt asked.

"Not even a hint," Emily said, grinning as she held to the hand of a squirming toddler. Her husband bent down and swooped the boy into his arms. "When we had lunch together yesterday, all she could talk about was the family Labor Day picnic and how excited and blessed she felt to be a part."

"No hints from me, either," Madison said. "And man, was it hard!"

"She still thinks the two of you are going for pedicures after her show, right?" Lawson asked his niece, who had mellowed considerably in their months together. Not that they didn't have their moments and head-butts, but he didn't regret a second of making her part of his life.

"Of course, Uncle Sheriff." There went those rolling eyes. "I did my part."

"Perfect."

Gazing around at the people collected inside the conference room of Calypso Radio, Lawson's chest swelled with pleasure. The Caldwell clan was here. Every member of the family, including extended members, had embraced Dallas completely. She was part of them, and they were here for her big surprise. At least, he hoped it was a surprise and not a disaster. He got the jitters thinking about it, but with lots of help from family and coworkers, he'd orchestrated this special event.

The station manager, Bill Jacobs, who'd helped put this gig together, stepped into the room. Every voice hushed. So much so, that Lawson could hear his heart pounding. He could also hear Dallas through the speakers set up inside the conference room. She was doling out advice to a brokenhearted caller.

"You're up in three minutes, Sheriff." Bill handed off a cell phone. "You're all set to be patched straight through to Dallas."

A flock of birds fluttered around in Lawson's belly. Suddenly, his mouth was sandpaper dry.

Nate whacked him on the shoulder. "Go get 'em, cowboy."

So, he stepped out in the quiet hallway and made the most important call of his life.

DALLAS WATCHED the teleprompter and the engineer, Shelby, in the glass booth across from her microphone. Shelby must be dating someone special. She had a beautiful glow about her today as she worked the control panels and kept Dallas on schedule.

Shelby held up one hand, counting down until the music ended and the next caller was on the air.

When she reached one, Dallas took a breath and said, "A little soothing tune for Jamie's broken heart. Jamie, there's someone out there for you. Keep smiling, my friend, stay positive, and she'll find you."

A caller flashed on the screen. "Now, we're going to William, right here in Calypso. Good morning, William. What's going on with you today?"

"I'm calling to ask an important question."

Dallas sat up straighter, eyebrows tugged together. Lawson? Or someone named William with a very similar voice? "Ask away. *Daylight with Dallas* is here to help."

"Well, you see, I'm in love with an incredible woman, and I'm convinced she loves me too."

Dallas gave a warm, throaty chuckle. Lawson, for sure. What game was he playing at? "Sounds serious."

"It is. Very serious. So serious that she's got me thinking matrimony."

Her heart took one giant leap. What was he doing? What was she supposed to say to that?

Because she couldn't think what else to do, Dallas threw out the question she'd ask a regular caller. "Have you popped the question yet?"

"Actually, that's why I called."

In her peripheral vision, a sign appeared in the engineer's window. She lifted her eyes…lost her breath. Lawson was smiling through the glass, a cell phone to his ear. Madison held a poster board.

It said, *Please? We love you so much!*

"Dallas Langley," his wonderful, much loved voice said, "will you hitch your star to this small-town sheriff and make me the happiest man in the world? Will you marry me?"

"Lawson. Oh, Lawson." She completely forgot about the countdown to commercial and the end of her show. Her total focus was on the man in uniform with the bluest eyes she'd ever seen. Her love. Her man. Her perfect mate. Holding up a ring box.

Overjoyed, and so touched that he'd chosen this way to propose, she nodded up and down a dozen times. She, a woman who made her living with her voice, couldn't find it.

"Is that a yes?" he asked, and she could see his mouth moving.

"Yes, yes, yes." She tossed off the headphones, knowing Shelby would take over from there, and raced out of the booth. Lawson and a crowd of people met her in the hallway.

She jumped into Lawson's arms. He caught her,

stumbled back a step, only to be braced up by her brothers, every one of them grinning like maniacs.

She kissed him with all the love she had and received the same in return.

When she came up for air to applause and cheers, Dallas looked from Madison to Emily and the other Caldwell women and, finally, to Bethany and several friends from Bayville. "You knew? All of you?"

The answer came in smiles and nods. Madison jumped up and down in a fit of glee. Dallas couldn't believe the teen had kept a secret from her. They talked about everything. She pointed at the girl, whose grin was as big as a watermelon slice.

"Party in the conference room right now," Wyatt announced and spun around to lead the parade.

"How did you do this?" she asked in amazement as she and Lawson entered the party.

"Sneaky lawman." Lawson winked.

Balloons emblazoned with *Congratulations!* floated around the room. Huge signs graced the walls with her name and Lawson's in big red hearts. Madison's handiwork, no doubt. A cake and punch decorated one table. Gifts were on another.

"Lawson wanted to surprise you," Connie said, offering a side hug, the only kind she could give, considering that Dallas refused to leave Lawson's embrace.

"He certainly did that. I'm shaking all over." She held out a trembling hand.

"Other hand, please." Lawson stepped away and went to one knee. "Gotta make it official."

Suddenly a circle formed around them as if they'd all planned this moment.

Wonderful, incredible Lawson. He'd done this for her. Because he loved her that much.

"How did I ever find a man as thoughtful and romantic and fabulous as you?" Dallas asked.

"As I recall, you threw up on my sidewalk."

Laughter circled the room.

"Wait, wait." Lawson held a silencing hand toward the crowd. "That day, that moment, for me, was a blessing from God. You were beautiful and brave, trying so hard to be strong. When you collapsed in my arms, I never wanted to let you go. You were too beautiful for words, and I think I started falling in love with you right then."

Dallas offered her left hand. "You were my hero, my rescuer, and now you are my love."

"Then, to make this official, will you be my beautiful bride in sickness and health forever and ever?"

"I absolutely will."

He slid the ring on her finger, and, before she could move again, he clicked handcuffs on her wrist and attached the other to himself.

Dallas laughed and leaned in to seal the deal with a kiss.

Then, with a triumphant, "Yes!" Lawson lifted their locked hands toward the ceiling. Her engagement ring sparkled beneath the lights, a gorgeous diamond surrounded by sapphires the color of Lawson's eyes.

The room began to cheer and clap. Someone whistled. One of the babies squealed. So did Madison.

Dallas felt like squealing too. The surprise was perfect. The only thing that could have made it better was if her mother was here.

She clung to Lawson, not wanting to be sad.

Mom had taken the news better than Dallas had expected, finally explaining the circumstances surrounding Dallas's birth. Mom had met a grieving rancher, lonely and desperately in need of comfort, and had fallen in love. When she realized how much he still loved his late wife, Mom believed Clint could never love her the way she wanted and needed. After breaking off the relationship, she learned she was pregnant. Determined not to hurt the man she loved with demands, she kept her child a secret.

Dallas had taken comfort in the story. So had the Caldwell siblings. But her mother was still shy about meeting them.

"Hey." Lawson tapped her under the chin. "Where'd you go? Are you okay?"

Sweet, beloved man. Always thinking of her. "Very okay. But I wish my mom…"

The crowd parted and a slender blonde with Dallas's blue eyes came toward her, hands outstretched. "Baby."

"Mama." Suddenly, she was locked in a three-way embrace with Lawson doing his best to stay out of the way, even though they were handcuffed together. "You came. I didn't think…"

"Your beautiful new family drove all the way to Ft. Worth to meet me and make me feel welcome."

"They did?" she asked in wonder.

"They love you that much." Mom hitched her chin toward a grinning Lawson. "Especially that one. He threatened to arrest me if he had to."

Dallas shook her head in tender amusement. "Cops. What can I say?"

"I'll tell you what to say," Ace said above the noise. "Let's cut the cake!"

"Yeah," Madison said, her face glowing with excitement. "I'm starving."

Surrounded by family and friends, Dallas led the way to the engagement table, still handcuffed to the love of her life.

Joined. Connected. She and her cowboy sheriff. Not only by the wrists, but by the committed love inside their hearts, a love to last forever. Exactly the way God intended.

WHISPER FALLS

Rancher's Refuge

Baby in His Arms

Sugarplum Homecoming

The Lawman's Honor

REDEMPTION RIVER

Finding Her Way Home

The Wedding Garden

A Place to Belong

The Christmas Child

The Last Bridge Home

THE BROTHERS' BOND

A Season for Grace

A Touch of Grace

The Heart of Grace

Made in the USA
Middletown, DE
26 May 2020

96026163R00144